GAUGUIN'S MOON

T0154886

GUERNICA WORLD EDITIONS 18

GAUGUIN'S MOON

LAURA MARELLO

GUERNICA
World
EDITIONS
TORONTO—BUFFALO—LANCASTER (U.K.)
2019

Michael Mirolla, editor
Cover design: Allen Jomoc Jr.
Interior layout: Jill Ronsley, suneditwrite.com
Guernica Editions Inc.
1569 Heritage Way, Oakville, (ON), Canada L6M 2Z7
2250 Military Road, Tonawanda, N.Y. 14150-6000 U.S.A.
www.guernicaeditions.com

Distributors:
. University of Toronto Press Distribution,
5201 Dufferin Street, Toronto (ON), Canada M3H 5T8
Gazelle Book Services, White Cross Mills
High Town, Lancaster LA1 4XS U.K.

First edition.
Printed in Canada.

Legal Deposit—Third Quarter
Library of Congress Catalog Card Number: 2019930816
Library and Archives Canada Cataloguing in Publication
Title: Gauguin's moon / Laura Marello.
Names: Marello, Laura, author.
Series: Guernica world editions ; 18.
Description: Series statement: Guernica world editions ; 18
Identifiers: Canadiana (print) 20190052929 | Canadiana (ebook) 20190052937
| ISBN 9781771834315
(softcover) | ISBN 9781771834322 (EPUB) | ISBN 9781771834339 (Kindle)
Classification: LCC PS3613.A7394 .M37 2019 | DDC 813/.6—dc23

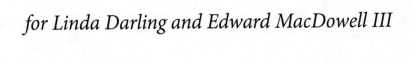

for Linda Darling and Edward MacDowell III

The dead are still looking at us, steadily, waiting for us to acknowledge our part in their murder.

—Harold Pinter

PART ONE

Visit from the Ancestors

I Play Bingo with My Ancestors

California, 1996

FOR THE FIRST few years after my mother died, I would go to sleep at night and dream my mother had come back. There were three versions of the dream. In the first, she would come back for a short visit. She made it clear she was still dead and could only visit for a few weeks. In the second version my mother would come back, again for a short visit, but she wasn't dead, she was alive. After a week or two she would get sick and die again.

In the third version I drove a car, and my mother rode in the passenger seat. But we weren't really on a road. Around us it rained, buildings and trees were on fire; the ground opened up around us; flaming debris fell from the sky; people, animals, and carts were headed in every direction. I gripped the wheel and said: *I'll get you out of here. I'll get you out of here.* Then I would wake up.

I never dreamed my mother was simply alive. I never dreamed she hadn't really died, or that she had come back from the dead for good and would not leave me again. I wondered then why I never dreamed it this way. If I could have her back at all, why couldn't I have her back for good? Some time in my late teens the dreams about my mother stopped. I haven't had any since.

I was forty before I actually saw my mother again. You can imagine my surprise. I had come home late from the studio and there she was, sitting on the futon couch with her knees together, waiting for me. She was quick to warn me that she was just there for a short visit, but I already knew that. I hadn't dreamed about her in over twenty years, but I could remember those dreams.

In real life my mother never sat on the couch with her knees together. She sat at the kitchen table drinking coffee and smoking cigarettes. She wasn't the right age now either. She looked around fifty. She was forty when she died, and she would have been seventy if she had lived. Fifty didn't make sense at all. I asked her about this and she said: *I don't make the rules.* I asked her if I were going crazy, if she were a hallucination. But she said: *Don't be silly*, and waved her hand at me. My mother always hated melodrama. She preferred a no-nonsense approach to life. I asked her if other people could see her and she said: *Of course, I'm your mother, come for a visit.*

But everyone knows you're dead.

We'll work something out.

I asked her if my sister knew she was here and she said no. I asked her if she was going to visit my sister and she said no. *But when she finds out you're here she'll want to see you*, I said. She said if I told my sister she was there she would have to leave abruptly and would never be able to return.

Mom, this is really complicated.

Indeed it is, she said. She did not appear fazed by this.

I asked her if she was hungry and she said she was. I asked her if this meant she was a real person at least while she was visiting.

Like a real person, she said. I asked her if I could touch her, then. She said: *Oh, I'm sorry*, and stood up from the couch, as if she had forgotten to greet me. She hugged me and that made me cry, so she held me for a while. That made me feel like a small child, which made me cry more. *There, there*, she said, and patted me on the shoulder, the way she had done when she was alive.

When I woke up the next day, I remembered what had happened the night before as an interesting new twist on my old dreams. But if I had been dreaming, I still was. My mother was in the kitchen, brewing strong coffee and scrambling eggs. *I don't eat eggs!* I said, horrified.

My mother gave me a bemused look. *They're not for you,* she said. She asked me what I ate now.

You don't know?

I'm not clairvoyant, she said. I didn't remember my mother ever using words like clairvoyant before. I wondered how much she'd changed since she'd been dead. My mother asked me if I remembered what I used to eat for breakfast, when I was young and so afraid of everything it made my stomach hurt. I remembered: she'd tempt me with a glass of chocolate milk, and at the last minute, she would whip a raw egg into it.

I sat down at the dining room table, looked out at the bay, and wondered why my mother had come to visit me from the dead. Was she trying to assist me at a difficult moment? This moment in my life did not strike me as more difficult than others. In some ways it seemed easier, now that I had an ongoing job and had finished a body of work. On the other hand, I had just turned forty; for the last ten years I had a back injury that kept me in chronic pain, had ruined my finances and threatened to put me out of work altogether, and I had not yet had a major show of my artwork.

What do you want for breakfast? my mother was asking me.

Rice cereal, I said. I asked her why she was making eggs.

I didn't come alone, she said. *The others are in the living room.*

I wondered whom she would bring with her. Would they be dead or alive? Her closest ties, or mine? I went into the living room. My great Aunt Charlotte—the most important dead person in my life after my mother—was sitting on the futon couch, staring into the fireplace, where someone had built a nice fire. She immediately got up, hugged me and said: *It's good to see you darling*, in her southern accent. She was the same in every respect as when I had seen her in Manhattan thirty years before, when she had been an international buyer for Gimbel's and lived on the Upper West Side. She smelled the same—like Houbignant; dressed the same—in her Chanel suit with her blonde hair in the French twist; had the same warmth, the same timbre of voice, the same affectionate nature. She hadn't aged—she still looked around sixty.

My first lover, Elaine, the most important dead person in my life after my mother and Charlotte, was sitting in the rocking chair. When I saw her she got up, said hello in her awkward way, and gave me a quick hug. She too looked about the same as when I had last seen her ten years before: thin, blonde, gray eyes, jeans, t-shirt, around forty. Except she looked healthy—not terminally ill from breast cancer.

So we were the same age—at last. When I fell in love with her I had been a teenager; she was married and in her mid twenties, just out of the University of Southern California film school. We met working on the same film—she was assistant directing, I was a high school intern working with the art director. I'd never felt like I was on equal terms with her.

So the three most important people in my life, all of them dead, were now in my house. I was sure I had gone crazy when I noticed Andrew standing on the porch. He was shirtless, smoking a Gauloise, and cradling a glass of Glenlivet on the wooden porch rail, his turquoise bracelets jangling on his wrist. He stared out at the bay.

When I met Andrew I was a teenager and still in love with Elaine. Andrew was a Los Angeles banker turned furniture restorer who lived in the high desert above Palm Springs amongst pre-Colombian and Egyptian art objects, healing the wounds from his lover Duane's suicide. In the 1970s and 80s, and until Andrew died, I had the distinction of being his only female friend. Wealthy people paid him millions to turn their modern furniture into wormwood and fake marble antiques.

I went out on the porch. Andrew had died of a brain tumor at fifty, bucking the trend of my mother and Elaine to die at forty, but keeping with the general tendency of Aunt Charlotte, and anyone else I truly cared about, to die before I had turned thirty. He turned from the view to look at me. *Hello gorgeous,* I said.

Hello beautiful, he said. He smiled at me, took a drag on his cigarette and sipped his scotch.

When you're dead you get to drink at eight in the morning? I said to him.

Andrew toasted me and laughed. *I'm in heaven,* he said. He put out his cigarette, opened the sliding glass door for me, and carried his scotch back inside.

Some party, I said. Aunt Charlotte and Elaine were relaxing by the fire, and talking amiably. When they saw me they got up and went into the dining room. We set the table. Andrew fixed himself another scotch and arranged some orchids and baby's breath in a vase on the table. He lit some vanilla candles. Aunt Charlotte and Elaine brought breakfast to the table: rice cereal for me; bacon, eggs and sausage for Andrew; pancakes for Mom and Aunt Charlotte; waffles with fruit for Elaine.

Needless to say, I had never seen my mother, Aunt Charlotte, Elaine and Andrew in the same room. They were all stylish people— my mother and Aunt Charlotte in the 1940s, Upper West Side, Chanel/ Houbignant, *we've won-the-war-and-dominated-Europe* sort of way; and Andrew and Elaine in the 1980s, Laurel Canyon, Calvin Klein and Armani, *greed-isn't-good-but-it-looks-good* sort of way. I wondered if the style and beauty I was familiar with from living with my mother and Aunt Charlotte had drawn me to Elaine and Andrew.

You were never this quiet, Aunt Charlotte said.

I'm stunned, I said, *like a deer caught in the headlights.* I asked her about her pancakes. She said they were excellent.

Elaine said: *Daniella was always quiet, but usually rather sullen as well,* and that her waffles were exquisite. She thanked my mother for making them. Andrew also thanked my mother and winked at me.

Why are you here? I said. *I must have gone crazy.* They laughed and assured me I hadn't. *I could be dreaming,* I said. They shook their heads. *Well then,* I said, *I must be dying.* Since my mother died, I had always been convinced that I would die at forty like she and Elaine had, that I would not outlive them. My sister confessed to me that she had had the same fear.

Of course you're not dying, Aunt Charlotte said. My mother concurred. They both seemed offended.

Then someone close to me is dying, I said. After all, that was the general trend, for anyone close to me to die young and tragically. Of course, I had put a stop to that: no one was close to me anymore.

No one's dying, my mother said.

So, I've just turned forty, I said, *and contrary to my own beliefs, I'm going to live through it*?

Bingo, Andrew said.

This is the more germane issue, my mother said. I thought she would go on to explain why she was using words like clairvoyant and germane, and why Aunt Charlotte and Andrew were there, but my mother had always been extremely laconic, and I had always pestered her with questions.

So what happens now? I said.

We'll visit you, my mother said.

What do we tell people? I said. *We can't very well tell them this is my mother come back from the dead for a visit.*

I could be your aunt, my mother suggested.

What aunt? I said. *I haven't seen my family in thirty years and suddenly I have aunts?*

I could be your aunt, Elaine said and guffawed.

I could be your aunt, Andrew said, and winked at me. *I am in France.*

I am your aunt, Aunt Charlotte said. *What's the harm in that?* She looked around defensively, but no one responded.

We'll figure something out, my mother repeated. *What would you usually do now?*

This morning? I said, astonished and alarmed.

This very morning, my mother said.

I'd work at the studio, I said.

So right now you go to the studio and work on your art, my mother said. *Business as usual.*

This sounded strange to me, as if they had an infinite amount of time. *How long are you staying?* I said.

We'll stay until we finish our visit, my mother said mysteriously. Aunt Charlotte shrugged. Elaine looked at the ceiling. Andrew took out his cigarettes and placed an unlit one into his mouth.

Where will you sleep? I asked.

We can manage our own accommodations, my mother said. They looked at her and smiled, as if they were relieved she was the spokeswoman for the group, as if there was something they weren't telling me.

For the first time in my life, I doubted her on all counts. They must have read it in my expression because they laughed. Elaine and Andrew had often enjoyed a joke at my expense, but never my mother or Charlotte. I thought that they were much more cheerful now that they were dead, except for Aunt Charlotte, who had always been cheerful.

Breakfast was over. I helped Andrew clear the table, and Elaine wash the dishes. No one asked or offered to do anything; no one bargained, negotiated or arranged; they all just did things, as if they knew what to do. This gave the atmosphere a peaceful, soothing, harmonious quality, as if everything was as it should be, and made me feel calm and secure. I liked having them all there, despite the fact that I had lived alone for twenty years, and wasn't accustomed to anyone cooking in my kitchen or washing dishes in my sink.

When the dishes were washed, dried, and put away, they all looked at me, as if I were expected to do what I was supposed to do—go to the studio and work. But I didn't want to go to the studio and work, I wanted to stay and visit with them.

There will be plenty of time for visiting, my mother said. *You must go on with your life as usual. Don't let us disrupt you.*

Sure, I said. *Just some dead people visiting for breakfast, nothing disruptive in that. I'll go right to the studio, breeze in, make a few sculptures. My concentration hasn't been broken. My focus hasn't been challenged.*

You have to admit she has a point, Andrew said. He sucked on the unlit cigarette he had placed in his mouth. I wondered why he craved cigarettes. Was there no separation between body and soul? Were bodily addictions so much a part of you that they lingered ten years after your death? Or, when you needed your body back, did the addictions come back with them? After my back surgery one of the

17

surgeons told me that once he started practicing, and saw how the body functioned so mysteriously, and so entirely without our conscious control, he became convinced that we were merely renting out our bodies, inhabiting them. I wondered. I knew body and soul were somewhat independent and autonomous, but in some ways they also seemed inextricably linked. It was a paradox to me.

My mother said: *It's like school when she was little. If she'd lived alone as a child she'd have gone off to school every day without a problem. But she had to leave us. If she never had to leave anyone, Daniella would be able to do anything.*

I remembered it very well. Every morning my stomach would ache. My sister would leave for school before me. I would try to convince my mother that I was dreadfully sick, and could not possibly even make it to school, much less stay there for six or seven hours. My mother would tell me I was just afraid, which was true, and that once I got there I would enjoy it, which I did. I loved school. In the meantime, I still had to leave her, and my chin would quake and I would start to cry because what she said was true. She would kiss my forehead, wipe my tears away with her fingertips, and make me go. She always made me go.

Perhaps that was why as a child I so liked that story *Pippi Longstocking*. She was nine and lived alone. Her father had left her some money—a chest of gold coins—which she kept at the foot of her bed.

She could take the day off, Aunt Charlotte suggested. She slipped me a chocolate covered marzipan in a gold wrapper. Aunt Charlotte had always tried to make me feel better about myself rather than insist I face my fear. My clearest memory of it was when I was six years old and supposed to go to a birthday party. I remember the yellow dress and the wrapped present in my hand. I was crying; I didn't want to go. Aunt Charlotte could not bear to see me cry, so she suggested I stay home. My mother insisted I go. I went, and had a wonderful time. I was only afraid of the unknown, of the unimaginable future. If the present came, and I was forced to act, I often acted without fear.

This fear had stayed with me throughout my life. It started before I could remember. I don't know what triggered it. I never knew what caused it. My sister told me that when I was born I was 22 inches long, weighed only five pounds, and they didn't put me in the incubator. Sometimes I wondered if that made me feel unprepared for what was to come.

In elementary school I wouldn't use the cafeteria, because I had never gone inside and seen it. I didn't know what was inside there, or how to use it. I was too afraid to go in and find out. In high school I was too afraid to go to a football game or to change planes in Atlanta to visit my grandmother. But I would do huge, reckless things, like drive across the country at sixteen. Or I would do bold, romantic things, like live alone in Paris for a year when I was in college. Of course once there I was afraid to go to dinner parties, or cross the Channel to England. In my thirties I could remain perfectly calm and motionless, and even watch the monitor while doctors inserted long needles into my spinal discs, or face life-threatening back surgery, and afterward move alone from California to upstate New York to take a college teaching job, but I was afraid to leave the house once my back healed, and I was afraid to speak in public once I'd taken the job.

The contradictions baffled everyone, including myself. My sister said she would have been too frightened to live alone in Paris, or face life threatening surgery, or move from California to upstate New York for a job, but she could go to a football game, she could leave the house, and she could speak in public.

I understood it this way: The football game (or the cafeteria, or the job) and Paris were equally scary to me, because they were both new. But Paris was worth it; the football game wasn't. When my car blew up I wasn't scared because it happened too fast. Then it was over. When I had to have six hours of back surgery where five doctors opened up my abdomen and journeyed through my entire body to get to my back, I wasn't scared. I figured if they burst a vein and couldn't sew it up in time I wouldn't be awake to know I was dying. I had never been afraid of death anyway. Death seemed like I way out. It was living that terrified me.

Sometimes I calculated the diversity in my life in descending order: I have slept with sixty-two people, fifty men, and twelve women. I have moved forty-eight times, worked twenty-one jobs, I have lived in eight towns. I have created hundreds of photographs and sculptures that have never been shown in galleries. I have never had a job or a residence for more than three years, a relationship for more than one. I have never been on a vacation. I travel on airplanes twice a year, but always alone. The last time I was on an airplane with someone I knew was over thirty years ago. People wonder why I am afraid to move again, start another job, start another relationship, take another trip, speak in public, make a new friend, drive in traffic. Isn't it obvious?

What I don't understand is why the fear was always there. My life just exacerbated it. What caused that fear? Where did it come from? Sure, there's the low-birth-weight baby theory, and the anxious parents theory, and the 50s baby boomer generation performance-is-everything theory. Any of those is enough to create anxiety that starts before you can remember. But something is missing here—some piece of information that would explain it to me. I know it shouldn't matter why I'm afraid, or why I started out that way. It matters more that I face my fear, and learn to manage it. But I want to know why. I want to know why, from before I can even remember, I have always been afraid.

I preferred Aunt Charlotte because she did not force me to face my fears. But I also preferred her because Aunt Charlotte leaned toward sensuality and opulence, where my mother believed in pragmatism and asceticism; because Aunt Charlotte had encouraged and believed in my photography and sculpting before anyone else had; and because my cousin insisted that during her jet set life in the fashion industry in the 1940s, Aunt Charlotte had had affairs with other women.

Maybe we'll drop by the studio, my mother said. She kissed me goodbye and stood at the door. I looked at Elaine, Andrew and Aunt Charlotte. Andrew tried to look reassuring but he seemed more amused than empathetic, and that did not console me. Elaine just smirked at me, and tried to look bored. Any show of emotion made her uncomfortable. Aunt Charlotte looked stricken by my pain, empathetic to a fault, and it was almost worth going, just so that she would feel better.

The bottom line was that I didn't trust them. I knew they were just a bad dream or a figment of my imagination and they would disappear as soon as I took my eyes off of them. When I was a child, my mother thought experience would teach me that when I left a person, I would see them again in a few hours, after my mother got back from the grocery store or I returned home from school. But I knew better. When I was seven, we moved from New York to Los Angeles, and I almost never saw Aunt Charlotte again. When I was twelve I lost my mother. When I was thirty I lost Elaine and Andrew. When I was thirty-one I hurt my back, and my life had never been the same since. I even lost myself. My worst fears had all been realized.

But my mother seemed to be running things, and there was no changing her mind, so I took my keys, smiled, said goodbye, and left. My mother stood at the open door and watched me until I had walked down the stairs and was out of sight, the way she had done when I had started off to school as a child. She had packed me a lunch brown paper sack, which I carried it in my hand as I went. This increased my feeling of childlikeness. But I always felt like a child these days, somewhere between the ages of four and eight. I pretended I was a grown up to work or do my art or be around people, but when I really felt something, I felt small, vulnerable, and hurt; or awestruck, amazed, and delighted; or mischievous, devilish, and impish.

I had become Pippi Longstocking in a way—a small child who, for twenty-three years, daily renewed her delight in being free to live alone and do what she liked—except no one had left me any money, and I felt woefully unable to earn it myself. That was part of the fear. I was afraid I couldn't take care of myself, and no one was going to help me, or do it for me. Certainly nothing in my life so far indicated I could take care of myself, since I had not yet been successful at jobs, career, relationships.

On my way to the studio I lapsed into a morass of self-loathing and self recrimination. I told myself the dead relatives weren't coming to the studio. I told myself breakfast had been the entire visit, and when I returned home in the evening, they would all be gone. I berated myself for not staying with them. It was bad enough I had lost them once. At least I had been young then and hadn't understood the pain of loss, or the discomfort of unfinished business. Now I was afraid I had lost them *twice*. But the marzipan chocolate was still in my pocket. I wondered if they really would stay for awhile. It seemed a highly optimistic idea.

I wanted to call my friend Sandy to tell her what happened, so she could tell me I really had gone crazy now, and needed to seek help, but my model was coming in an hour, and I had to set up my work and get everything ready before she got there.

I was working on a series of half-reclining nudes in terracotta. They were large, and composed of rounded and cylindrical shapes, big almond eyes, their hair pulled back, their toes curled in delight, their palms outstretched. They were more Oceanic than European, a Maillol in Hawaii. My California influences were reasserting themselves through a severe bout of homesickness that seemed to take me even further west, to the Pacific Islands. I needed light. I needed warmth. I needed the Pacific. So I made the half-reclining terracotta women. It was important to me that they were half reclining—not completely reclining or completely upright. They were neither here nor there—like me.

And I was working on a series of silver-tint photographs of nudes half-submerged in sand and water. I called these *Body Landscapes*. The curves of the hips echoed the curves of the dunes. The dappled water mimicked the dappled flesh. The grainy sand resonated in the grainy skin. Like the half-reclining terracottas, these bodies were neither completely in nor out of the water, neither completely submerged in sand, nor on top of it. Where were they going? No one knew. When people asked me what my work was all about I didn't know what to tell them—sex, bodies, beauty, the ocean, peace, languor, comfort, respite, sunlight, homesickness, the search for oblivion.

I unwrapped my clay and wheeled it into position when I heard a knock at the studio door. It was too early for my model or my dead relatives. I opened the door. It was Sandy.

Sandy had been my friend for the past twenty years. When we'd met in college. A mutual friend, who was running the Friday night Ingmar Bergman Film series on campus, introduced us during the screening of the *Seventh Seal,* while the hero was playing chess with Death.

Sandy was an onomatopoeia. She looked as her name suggested— sandy. Her hair was light browns, blondes, her eyes hazel and flecked with green, her skin tawny and freckled. If you took her to the beach she blended in, like camouflage. And she was sparkly, glittery, like the light reflecting off the beach surfaces. She had recently moved from San Francisco to Boston, because her husband, who taught astrophysics, had left Berkeley for MIT. They had decided to summer on the Cape, despite her husband's insistence that the beach was too bright, and the Cape too decadent. But Sandy needed the light; she was a painter. So they came.

I called your house, Sandy said. *Your mom answered.*

I nodded. So it was a group hallucination now.

You told me your mom died when you were twelve, Sandy said.

She did, I said. I explained to her what had just happened.

What does everyone look like? she asked. *What did they say at breakfast? Why did Andrew and Elaine come?*

I told her a few of the details. I told her my mother seemed to be the only one who had changed, the other three seemed the same as before.

You seem oddly restrained, Sandy said. *I think if my dead relatives came to visit, I would get excited.*

It was probably true. I was often oddly restrained. I thought I was numb. People who didn't know me thought I was lacking in affect. People who knew me thought I was avoiding things. But then, at other times, I was oddly emotional: too angry, too hurt, too affectionate, too intense, too in love, too preoccupied, too worried. Usually it was my lovers, my ex lovers and my potential lovers who pointed this out to me.

Sandy had no dead relatives, and no dead ex lovers. In fact, she had never even been rejected by any of her ex lovers. In matters of love Sandy was not a reckless, self-sabotaging risk-taker like me. I thought of her as someone who had protected herself well, who had not yet been affected by loss. Sometimes it made me afraid for her. Other times I thought she had been wise to protect herself against loss and rejection in the ways that I had not.

But we can't always prepare. I woke up one morning to find that my mother was dying. She blindsided me. I had no warning. I didn't see it coming, so I had no reason to prepare. I could only face it afterward, which I never did. Once hurt, or criticized, or rejected—I ran for cover. Evaded. Withdrew.

Now I spent my time anxiously anticipating the unknown, as if this were the same as protecting one's self against or preparing for the unknown. I must have thought that the more anxious I was beforehand, the better prepared I was, the less likely I'd be blindsided again. Of course that wasn't true. You can always get blindsided. No matter how anxious you are, no matter how much you prepare, now matter how you try to protect yourself, something unexpected always could happen. Your dead relatives could show up, for example.

I know, I said.

So what's the problem? Sandy said.

Sandy, what if they're not real? I said. *What if I'm imagining them? I mean no one has seen them but me.*

Sandy said: *If they're not real someone is over at your house doing very good impressions of their voices.*

It's nice of you to believe in me, I said, *but what if I've gone crazy? Maybe I made them up.*

Then how could I hear them?

Maybe it's a group hallucination. Maybe because you've known me for twenty years you became involved in the hallucination with me. It's contagious—like The Plague Of The Biting Nuns.

What plague of the biting nuns?

I said: *Some nuns started biting each other in Germany in the 1500s and it spread all over Europe.*

Oh please, Sandy said. *Do you want me to go over there?*

Maybe we should send someone neutral. A pizza delivery guy or something. Someone who wouldn't be susceptible to group hallucination.

I'm going over there. I'll call you later and tell you what happened. She picked up her keys. *But first tell me one thing. You said when you came home last night and when you got up this morning the dead relatives were in the apartment. How did they get in? Do you keep the doors unlocked?*

I lock the doors. I have no idea how they got in.

Well, maybe you should make them a set of keys, Sandy said.

The Heart Song Man

I STARTED SCULPTING WHEN I was seven. It began this way: We had to make something for the Los Angeles County Schools Science Fair. I wanted to make a mechanical man. I wanted him to walk and talk, make my breakfast, water the lawn, adjust the chlorine levels in the new pool. Looking back on it now, I imagine I wanted to make a robot, but I didn't know what a robot was. It was 1963. We had just moved from New York to Los Angeles.

I rummaged around in the garage, where my father kept his supplies. My father was an architectural draftsman who designed department store interiors for the 1960s shopping-mall boom in Los Angeles. He had submitted elaborate design plans to the family twice: once for a doghouse, and again, after we saw the movie version of Rodgers and Hammerstein's *Oklahoma*, for a surrey. So there was always an assortment of wood, screws and nails around.

But my father had also been a radio operator in the Aleutian Islands during World War II, and had installed a highly byzantine intercom system in our four-bedroom ranch house. He possessed an assortment of electrical wire, copper wire, chips, circuit boards, crystals, knobs, plates, backings, rubber feet, and other oddities, squirreled away in tiny boxes that were neatly labeled in his angular architect's handwriting. This cache fascinated me more than the wood, and it was from it that I set out to make my mechanical man.

What I ended up with, of course, was a metal sculpture, not a robot. It was my first experience with the discrepancy between intention and result, and the longing produced by unsatisfied desire.

But I put a little music box in his chest, where his heart should be, to make his heart sing. This gave me pride. Though the *Heart Song Man* had nothing to do with science, he won second prize at the fair.

Making the *Heart Song Man* was a revelation to me. It was the first time I did something that made me feel like myself. I wasn't afraid; I wasn't anxious; I didn't care what anyone thought. I was peaceful, content, happy, playful, mischievous, euphoric even. From then on, whenever I made something that was useless, except to communicate what my soul imagined, I felt like that—like myself.

Afterward, I always wanted to make things, because I always wanted to feel that way. My father tried to encourage me to make things that were "useful," but for some reason the things he wanted me to make—buildings, intercom systems, lawn sprinkler systems, etc.—seemed less useful to me than what I wanted to make. I wanted to make a batik painting of a large water beetle in purples and reds. I wanted to make an acrylic painting of the crab mosaic I had seen in the tunnel at Jones Beach when I was three. I wanted to recreate that feeling of the sand on the cold concrete, the dark-damp, the echoes, the feeling that the sun was just up ahead and at any moment it would burst down on you like a piece of over-ripe fruit splitting open. Nobody understood this, and I lacked the ability to explain it to them.

But my sister did something for me, without realizing it. She showed the *Heart Song Man* to my mother. My mother was at the grocery store when I finished it. Before my mother got home, my sister happened upon the *Heart Song Man,* and with her usual dovetailing of exuberance and good will, fawned over it. *How Marvelous!* she had said, *How Lovely! How Delightful!* as if each word was capitalized and had an exclamation point after it. When my mother drove up in the turquoise Rambler, my sister wouldn't even let her take the groceries out of the car. She took my mother's hand. *You have to come look*, she said. *It's Incredible! It's Terrific!* It occurred to me she was using all the words that the spider had used to describe Wilbur the pig in *Charlotte's Web*.

My sister told my mother I had made the *Heart Song Man* myself. *Isn't it amazing?* my sister said.

She couldn't have made it herself, my mother said. She walked around the garage work table, looking at it from all angles. I turned the music box on so my mother could listen to his heart sing.

But she did! my sister said. *She's a genius!*

You must have helped her, my mother said. She looked at me like I was a Martian. I smiled congenially at her.

I didn't help her! my sister said. *I came in the garage and here it was!*

My mother examined me again. *Well,* she said, *that's quite an accomplishment. What is it?*

We told her it was the *Heart Song Man.* When it won second prize my sister felt her belief in me was confirmed, and this gave her a sense of moral triumph. My mother, on the other hand, looked reassured. She looked a little less afraid.

How to Manage
Passion and Borrow Birds

WHEN MY MODEL arrived I positioned her in the chair on the modeling stand and went to work. She was patient as always, but asked me if perhaps something was wrong? Was I distracted? I said I wasn't, but I could not stop thinking about my mother, and wondering why, if I wasn't dying, and no one else I knew was dying, she and the others had come to visit me. Had they come to help me with my job? My career? My back injury? To help me start a relationship? Face my fears?

The thought was fleeting; it could not have occupied more than a few seconds; but when I looked up, my model was gone, and instead my mother was on the stand, seated, as if she were modeling—except that she was fully clothed, as I suppose a mother should be.

Where's the model? I said.

I sent her home, Dear, my mother said. She got up from the modeling seat and wandered around the studio, looking at the sculptures of half-reclining women in terracotta and the photographs of women half-submerged in sand and water. She did not seem pleased, but maybe I was reading too much into it.

When? I said. *I only looked down for a second.*

There's an infinity of time in a second. Anyway, you've never functioned at the same speed as other people. Do you remember that time when you were eight and you came into the laundry room to tell me that everything was going too fast?

I remembered it. The world around me had become like a video tape on fast forward, except it was the 1960s and there was no video tape then. I didn't know how to explain it, and at the time, my mother did not understand.

But I didn't hear anything, Mom, I said. *What did you tell her?*

You were absorbed in your work. Don't trouble yourself about it.

My mother continued to wander around the studio. She began to touch the sculptures lightly, with her fingertips, as if she were remembering something.

How did you get in? I said. *Sandy said I should make you a set of keys.* My mother looked up from the half-reclining terracotta woman she was examining, as if she had been called away.

That's very thoughtful, Dear, but it won't be necessary, my mother said. She sat down in a chair next to the sculpture I had been working on when my model was there.

You have to get in Mom. I'm not always there. You can't leave the apartment door unlocked when I'm sleeping or in the shower, like you did when you went to the grocery store.

We won't, my mother said. *We didn't.*

But how did you get in and out? I said. *Did you borrow my keys?*

If you must know, she said, *we're not solid. We came through the door.*

But you ate! I said.

We didn't want you to eat alone.

Mom! I thought you were like real people.

We are, she said. *When you're there, we'll knock. If you're out, or asleep, or showering—*

How will you know? I said.

We know.

Can you see through things? I said. *Can you see me when I'm alone, or with other people?* I tried to think of all the thoughts I wouldn't have wanted her to know, all the conversations I wouldn't have wanted her to hear, and all the meetings I wouldn't have wanted her to witness.

You've always had your privacy, she said.

Privacy! I said. *What do you know?*

Only what most people know. Only what groups of people can and do know.

Groups? Which groups?! I said, alarmed. *Name names!*

Look, don't trouble yourself with the details. We'll use the keys, alright? It was very nice of Sandy to suggest it. I was just trying to save you some trouble.

Trouble! I said. *You're not going to walk through walls in front of us, are you?*

Doors, my mother said, as if her sensibilities had been offended. *Of course not. We're not solid, that's all. We can't watch you, we can't overhear your conversations, we can eat—but we don't need to. We're not solid,* she repeated.

I'm not solid either, I said.

I knew about these things. As a small child I had been obsessed with various branches of the sciences. In the first grade dinosaurs enthralled me. I studied the different kinds and made replicas of them out of kits. When I had mastered them I went on to investigate the Saber Tooth Tiger, the Woolly Mastodon, and the Pterodactyl. I became the local expert on prehistoric animals in my neighborhood, and any boy or girl within several blocks who was preparing a report or building a model came by my home to consult me. I made frequent trips with grade school classes to the La Brea Tar Pits in Los Angeles, where dinosaur bones had been recovered, and even corrected some of the information they had presented in their exhibits there.

In the fourth grade I became an expert on rock formations. I collected specimens. I went hiking through the canyons with a backpack, a vest riddled with pockets, and a guidebook, and brought home as many kinds of rock as I could find. I speculated on the various geological and climatic conditions that had resulted in the unusual canyons on the Getty Oil land to the north of my housing tract, or the interesting rock hills near the Spahn Ranch to the west. I accumulated drawers and chests and shelves full of samples, all labeled and named and dated. I used weight and measurement and spectroscopic equipment at the local college to test my finds. When our family took trips I would point out the geological points of interest from the back seat of the Rambler or the Impala. They laughed and rolled their eyes.

In the sixth grade I immersed myself in a study of the neurophysiology of the brain. First I studied the different segments of the brain and how each part worked. Then I researched the neuro-pathways, synapses and connections. I studied dendrites and how they grew. I found out how information jumped over the gaps at the synapses in order to travel.

My zeal for research vanished while I was in junior high and high school, when I focused on boys, the visual arts, and eventually Elaine, but it reappeared in college, where I researched the neurochemistry of vision during dream sleep. I discovered that, even though no light enters the eyes, the rods and cones fire as if the eye is actually seeing something. I also learned that if kittens are raised in an environment where there are only horizontal lines, for example, when released into the larger world, they can see only horizontal lines. They've been conditioned to a limited viewpoint. What for an unconditioned kitten would simply be a chair leg, for them is a dangerous obstacle, because they can't see it. They'll run into it and anything vertical, anything they've been conditioned not to see. I've always thought this made a great metaphor for some truth about life, but I've never been able to figure out what exactly that truth is.

My chemistry professor was so moved by my enthusiasm for this research that he suggested I become a research chemist. When I told him I didn't think I could make it through organic chemistry, calculus and trigonometry, he offered to help me. I didn't think I could pursue it successfully without giving up my sculpture and photography, so I declined, but my passion for research persisted. Now it has focused on quantum physics. I am convinced that quarks and the bootstrap theory are setting out to prove everything the *I Ching* and the original texts of Hua Yen Buddhism revealed in 1500 B.C. Or anyway, that's my theory.

What do you mean you're not solid, my mother said.

Every year I replace most of my atoms, I said. *I replace my stomach lining every few days, my liver every few weeks, my skin every month, my skeleton every few months.*

That's true, she said.

So why can't I walk through walls?

Doors, my mother said. *Maybe you can.*

So what's the difference between me and you?

You're not dead yet, she said. *I am.*

It occurred to me that my mother had become very Zen since she'd been dead. I wondered if all dead people were Zen like her. I tried to imagine my father being Zen; he had been dead for only two years. I was having a difficult time. A few weeks after my mom died my father became exasperated with me one day and told me it was my fault my mother died, that I'd murdered her by asking so many questions. I knew it wasn't true. I knew she'd died of cancer. I knew he was just frustrated and angry and bitter and didn't mean me any harm. Still, I never forgave him.

I've been having dreams about Dad, I said.

What kind of dreams?

I dreamed he drove me to the airport in a white car. He was only twenty and was dressed in his army uniform; I was going back to California. I was angry with him because he was late, and when he parked the car he bumped the front fender on a light pole. Then when I got on the plane to actually go to California—

Is this still the dream? my mother said.

No, I said, *in real life, when I got on the plane, it was snowing and they couldn't take off. They kept us on the runway for two hours. I was going to miss my connection, so I didn't want to go. But they wouldn't let me off the plane. I remembered my dream and I didn't know if I should worry—that Dad had given me a warning—or if I should be calm, because Dad was telling me not to worry, that I'd be alright.*

So what happened? my mother said. *Obviously nothing bad; you're still here.*

*The plane never took off. The flight was canceled. We went back.
When I was waiting in the airport for a ride home I started crying
because I thought Dad had been trying to tell me not to worry, that
everything would be okay. And it was.*

Your father always wanted you to be safe and happy, my mother
said.

Sometimes I think he's a bird, I said.

What bird?

*Different birds. When he died there was a bird on the antennae on
the studio roof. A sparrow. I could see it through the skylight. It flew
away. So now when I see a bird in an odd situation, or at a particular
moment that strikes me as uncanny, like if it's right when I'm trying to
figure out what to do about something important, I think it's Dad trying
to tell me something.*

For example?

*For example, there were these two doves on the woodpile on the
porch. There are never doves on the porch. There are never doves anywhere around here. Then I saw them again out front. They were playing
a game with a cat, sitting on the road till the cat came too close, and
then flying up just out of reach. It drove the cat crazy. I thought maybe
they had a nest nearby and were protecting it, but for that a bird will
swoop down on a cat and spike it, not play a game with it. These birds
were sitting on the ground—proverbial sitting ducks. Then I saw them
again in a tree out back. Another time, at the beach, when I was trying
to decide whether to go on to Europe or back to California, this seagull
flew really low over me, made a loud noise, and headed straight for my
car. Birds never head straight for my car. It landed right on the hood,
flapped its wings twice, then took off again, east.*

And how do you interpret these signs?

*Well, the sparrow on the antennae I thought must have been Dad
saying goodbye. I don't have any idea what the doves on the woodpile
or teasing the cat meant, but I thought it was something about a relationship, since they seemed to be a couple. And the seagull on my car
hood was headed east, which might mean go to Europe, but it was also*

headed back up the Cape, which might mean go back to California, so I didn't know how to interpret that. What do you think, Mom? Does Dad like to appear to me in the form of birds?

Birds have always been regarded as messengers, my mother said evasively. I rolled my eyes at her. *Well, your father may have borrowed a bird or two now and then, but he's not every bird, dear.*

Borrowed? I said. *Borrowed?*

My mother smirked. She looked uncomfortable.

What do you mean, borrowed? I repeated, but I knew she wasn't going to tell me. *So what do the birds mean? And the dream?*

I don't know, honey. I don't have the answers.

You mean dead people don't have all the answers?

Only you have your answers.

Don't you hate when people say that? I said. *Everything you need is inside you. You just need to learn how to access it, how to use it. I feel like I'm in the end of* The Wizard of Oz *when Dorothy says she had a dream, and you and you and you were there, and if she ever goes looking for her heart's desire again she's sure she'll find it in her own backyard.*

Maybe it's true, my mother said.

Do you know how to use what's inside you? I asked.

No.

See. You're dead and you don't even know.

Dying doesn't enlighten you, necessarily. It's just another change. Everything's always changing.

We know how to harness the energy outside us—sunlight, electricity, sound waves, radio waves. So why don't we know how to use what's inside us?

That's a good point, she said.

You're dead. You're not solid anymore. But you've come back here and you look solid. So you must know something.

It's not that simple.

I was afraid of that, I said. I wasn't sure if she was being truthful, or holding something back, something she wanted me to find out for myself.

So I asked her what she did at the FBI. I had always wanted to know and no one in the family had ever been able to tell me. It was the only thing I had ever asked my family as a child that they had not been willing to at least try to explain to me. Due to the faulty workings of childhood logic, when I was young I became convinced that if I could find out what my mother did for the FBI, I could unlock the other mysteries of my childhood, like why I was afraid from before I could even remember. I guess I still believed it at forty.

A story had always circulated through our family that my mother had been chosen as part of ten high school graduates to work for the FBI in 1942, when she was sixteen. She was hired to work at the Washington D.C. office, but Aunt Charlotte wanted my mother to live with her, so she had her transferred to the New York City office.

My mother said it was all true, even the part about how, for the first few months, my mother used to smoke in Aunt Charlotte's bathroom, until Charlotte told her to stop hiding and smoke in the living room. It all sounded very glamorous to me, smoking, spying, the war, living in New York City.

Of course, these were all things that killed you.

But what did you do there? I repeated.

I can't say.

Why not?

It seemed to me that now that she was dead she could tell me anything. Certainly there were other things she had told me now that I didn't think she would have told me had she been alive.

It's top secret, she said. *It was war-time.*

But it's not war-time now.

For some reason I was sure that logic would appeal to dead people, that dead people were smarter, purer, more enlightened and evolved than living people.

It's still top secret, she said. *It hasn't been declassified.*

Did you type and file? I asked, hoping to get at it by process of elimination.

I don't type. I don't file. She sounded insulted.

Were you involved in information gathering?
You could say that.
Did you know things that were secret?
Are secret, she said. *Yes.*
Were you actually in the war? In Europe? Were you ever in danger?
I was never in Europe, my mother said. She didn't say that she had never been in danger.
Well that ruins my theory about my dream, I said.
What dream?
About driving you out of a war zone in a car. I told her about the dream; I described the landscape of rain and fire; flaming debris falling from the sky; the ground opening up; people, animals, and carts running in all directions. *I thought it was World War II, and you might have been there in real life.*
I wasn't in Europe.
Somehow I imagined that dead people, though they might speak in riddles or paradoxes like the Sphinx, would essentially speak clearly. I tried to put it out of my mind, but I kept thinking about my mother living on the Upper West Side with Aunt Charlotte. I envied her for that. When I was growing up my older sister was my mother 's favorite, and I was Aunt Charlotte's favorite. When my mother died Aunt Charlotte asked my father if I could come back to Manhattan and live with her, but he said no. No one told me she asked him, and he never asked me if I wanted to go. I saw Aunt Charlotte a few times after my mother's funeral, but after her husband died, she couldn't afford to visit Los Angeles, and I couldn't afford to fly to New York. When I was in high school, she died.
I had returned to Aunt Charlotte's West End Avenue apartment once, when I was in my mid-twenties. My cousin Ben and his partner had taken it over, and they let me stay in my uncle's old room. The apartment was at 79th and had a doorman. I still remembered the wooden griffins inlaid on the elevator door. For a month I lived on green salads and chocolate croissants from Zabar's. I took the crosstown bus to the East Side where I spent my days walking through

the Metropolitan Museum of Art, the Guggenheim and the Whitney. I attended gallery openings on 57th Street, and readings at the 92nd Street Y. I saw *Gandhi* at the Thalia, and went to lunch at the Algonquin.

I thought about what it would have been like to grow up on the Upper West Side, living with Aunt Charlotte. I would have gone to the Arts high school. She would have accompanied me to the Thalia and taken me to the film festival at Cannes. We would have summered on the French Riviera together, or in the Cyclades. She would have selected my perfume and chosen my wardrobe. She would have advised me about Elaine and Andrew. She would have encouraged me to study art at Pratt or Cooper Union.

Aunt Charlotte, Half Reclining

WHEN I LOOKED up, my mother was gone, and Aunt Charlotte was there in her place. She smiled at me, took off her clothes, and climbed up on the modeling stand.

Aunt Charlotte! I said.

It's all right, Dear. I'm dead. Dead people do and say all sorts of things they might not have done when they were alive. Besides, you're a grown up now.

My aunt had pushed the chair aside, and was half-reclined on the modeling couch, in the half-reclined position of terracotta women who were lounging around the studio.

And besides, darling, Aunt Charlotte said, *I'm only modeling.*

She was right; she was only modeling. I wheeled over a new block of clay and began. If there were any taboo against your aunt modeling for you, it didn't apply to a dead aunt.

Where's Mom? I said.

She went back to your apartment, Dear.

Why don't I see anyone come or go?

Don't worry Dear. It will all sort itself out in the end.

I nodded, though I was not entirely sure that it would. Breakfast had gone so smoothly, but the morning felt incredibly jerky, like watching a film that had not been properly threaded, or that had been repeatedly broken and re-spliced.

There was no one with you at the apartment this morning, Aunt Charlotte said. *Do you have a lover?*

I've had so many lovers, I said wistfully.

What were they like?

I wondered what to tell her. I was always attracted to blondes who looked like Aunt Charlotte, but who were restrained, tormented, pent up, brooding, full of unreleased emotion—like my mother. Like Elaine. Ice Queen blondes. Hitchcock blondes. Beginning with Andrew and Elaine, and until I was thirty, my lovers were mentors, artists of one sort or another. They helped me discover something about my work, but they were unavailable—not just emotionally, but physically as well. They were in other relationships, and they would leave me.

I often wondered why I had slept with so many people. Was I just a highly sensual or sexual person? A descendant of the Bonobos? Was I avoiding intimacy? Was I looking for intimacy and making the wrong choices? Was I a romantic risk taker? A serotonin, dopamine and phenylalanine addict? Had I been sexually abused and couldn't remember? Sometimes I accepted these explanations. Other times I suspected I was searching for oblivion, for comfort in the sensual, in the romantic, in passion, in obsession, and running away from my fear.

They seemed to be like you, I said, *but they were like Mom. I thought Elaine was like you, she's blonde—but she was restrained like Mom. I thought Andrew was like you—all the jewelry and artwork and the spirituality—but he was restrained, like Mom.*

A confusion of memory, Aunt Charlotte said. I nodded. *You need someone like me—someone who will give you unconditional love. Someone who will make you their favorite. Have you fallen in love recently?* I nodded. *You want people to enter into your dream with you, and that's good, but sometimes they can't.*

I looked at her. I was beginning to wish my aunt wasn't dead, and had never been my aunt.

Put it out of your mind, Dear. Aunt Charlotte said. She started laughing. I started laughing too.

Why is this so funny?

Laughter is anarchical. Don't try to understand it. Okay?

Okay, I said. I climbed up on the modeling stand and began to reposition her on the couch. She watched me.

Tell me what's wrong, she said.

Nothing's wrong.

Of course it is.

I sighed. How could I explain what was wrong? So many things were right. I lived at ocean part of the year, and I loved that. I had traveled to interesting places. I spent as much time on my artwork as I could, and I loved that too. But I had never had a relationship for more than a year, or a job for more than three years, or lived in one place for more than three years. I had never shown at the same gallery for more than a year. My work had never caught on. I earned enough money to get along, but I never had enough to buy adequate time to sculpt and photograph. I never saved any, I never had enough to invest in a house, or a car, or even a coat. It was as if I couldn't hang on to anything. I couldn't accumulate anything. And of course, I was always afraid. I was so tired of always being afraid. I told Aunt Charlotte this.

To accumulate things, you have to be able to hold onto them, Aunt Charlotte said.

I don't know how.

You have to build a container.

But how?

You'll see.

I don't understand.

You will. Don't worry about it now.

I'm afraid that I've become like Mom. People always said I was like you—warm, affectionate, childlike. Now they say I'm remote, withdrawn.

You'll change back.

When?

Soon, Aunt Charlotte said. Then she added: *Tell me what you know.*

This is what I know: I lost you when I was a child. If I don't let go I'll keep looking for you in people who are lost to me, like you are. And no

*matter where I go to look for you I won't find you, except inside myself,
because that's the only place you really are. But if I let you go, then I can
find someone like you—not because I want you back, or because I want
to replace you, but because I admire your qualities and want to be with
people who have them.*

Aunt Charlotte nodded. *There,* she said, *you understand part of it.
But I don't feel it in my heart. I don't believe it.*

You will.

I thought about the nightmare where I try to drive my mother
out of that apocalyptic landscape of rain and fire. In the dream I was
gripping the wheel and saying: *I'll get you out of here, I'll get you out
of here,* but we weren't going anywhere. If I drove forward we would
have fallen into a gaping hole in the earth or been hit by flaming debris falling from the sky and both been killed.

I told Aunt Charlotte about the dream. I asked her if my mother
had been in the war, really in it.

Stop worrying now, Aunt Charlotte said. *Was Rodin known before
he was forty?*

No.

Didn't he sleep with all his models?

Yes.

Come here, darling. She pulled on my arm. *I'll rub your back. I had
a bad back too, you know. Maybe you inherited that from me. A bad
memory.*

I sat down on the couch beside her. I wondered if my attraction
to blondes came from Aunt Charlotte. I had always been attracted
to blondes. In the first grade I fell in love with my blonde teacher. I
drew her pictures, wrote her poetry, and dreamed that I rescued her
from intruders by grabbing her around the waist and flying her out
the classroom window like I was Peter Pan. My first love was also my
first rescue fantasy.

In the fourth grade I fell in love with John Hernandez. He had
blonde hair, green eyes, and dark olive skin. He lived down the
block from us. I was obsessed with him, and for a year I kept a log of

everything he wore, drawing a colored diagram of each outfit. I could have been a child's clothing catalogue entrepreneur. But eventually Bo Didley moved in across the street from John, and I began to spend the afternoons between school and dinner at his house, listening to him play the Blues. Gradually my obsession faded.

In the fifth grade I went steady with Jim, a doe-eyed blonde who had six brothers and sisters, his own room, a maid and a pool. His father was an orthodontist, and his mother was a chemist. She kept frozen Snickers bars in the freezer for me.

In the sixth grade my schoolmates and I were all smitten with the tantalizing combination of Lucky Novo and his best friend Chance. Who knew what their real names were? Who cared? They were like every teenage heart throb movie actor of the last five decades rolled into one, from James Dean to Leonardo di Caprio.

In high school there was, of course, Elaine, and Andrew. But there was also Derek: tall, blond, handsome and voted most likely to succeed. Eventually he went on to drop out of UC Berkeley, but in high school he was the only boy my father was justified being suspicious of.

In college I fell in love with one of my art professors, a thin blue-eyed blonde from Yugoslavia. I sculpted my first clay bust of his head, but didn't sleep with him until I was in my late twenties. I also had my eye on a teenager who surfed the breakwater near my apartment building. Once he rode his skateboard inside my studio and sat and talked to me for a few minutes, then rode out again. He was an excellent surfer. He could ride up the underside of a wave, jump over the top, and spin around once before coming down the other side. They called that *cutting back*. When I tried it I fractured my skull. There is a photograph of him *cutting back* in the surfing museum at the lighthouse. I wish I had taken it myself.

In Paris I fell in love with Jean Louis Barrault in the 1942 film *Children of Paradise*, in his first mime scene, where he appears in the long blonde wig. All through graduate school I would search the newspaper listings of art film houses to see where that movie was playing. Luckily it became a cult film like *The Rocky Horror Picture Show*, and

I could always find a showing of it once or twice a year. When video tapes became available, I had to special order it. The video cost me a hundred dollars and came in two parts in a wide box. After a week I knew the movie by heart and could recite it, or hum the soundtrack, but mainly I said *Garance! Garance!* in a plaintive voice and held my hand to my throat.

I also fell in love with one of my Ecole des Beaux Arts professors, a buxom green-eyed blonde with flowing hair, who looked like she stepped out of a Rossetti painting. I had her over for dinner once, and I was so nervous I even asked the wine merchant on the corner to match my wine with my cheese for me. The next day I phoned her and told her that her perfume kept me company in my chair overnight and I was wondering if she would tell me its name. After that she had me over to her apartment every Wednesday afternoon, and invited me into the bathroom to sit with her while she prepared for her date with her doctor boyfriend. She would always spray a whiff of her Givenchy perfume on me before she left.

At the Art Institute, I had a brief affair with a large blue-eyed blonde from Nova Scotia who looked like a giant cupid in the shower. He liked to take me camping in the snow in his jeep (that he called Moose), so he could wipe ice off the windshield with his bare hands and tell me all Californians were sissies.

At Yaddo I met a very husky, older blonde, who did metal sculpture, and with whom I had a brief but torrid affair. He had taught at the New School for Social Research and had met Buckminster Fuller at Black Mountain College. We had a thirty-year age difference between us. At Montalvo Center for the Arts a bright-eyed, lean young blonde took me out to dinner, claiming he was twenty-three, but told me five years later he was just then twenty-three, and was really only eighteen the time before.

When I returned to Santa Cruz to recover from my back injury, I rediscovered my retired art professor, a blue-eyed, Boston-Irish blonde, who had studied at Radcliffe, and had that lovely Katherine Hepburn, *who-knows-where-it-comes-from-maybe-somewhere-in-Connecticut* accent. She was a very nervous, high-strung person, who was always darting about like a hummingbird.

The list went on. Blondes, blondes, blondes, I thought. Was it really Aunt Charlotte I had wanted all along? And if I just committed this tiny post-mortem act of incest, would it cure me, forever and always, of my desire for her?

Aunt Charlotte stroked my arm and hair. *Did Rodin have a bad back, darling?* she asked me.

No, I said. *Frida Kahlo.*

Blonde Ducks, Sitting Ducks

WHEN SHE WAS too tired to continue modeling, I said: *Can we do this again?*

Over my dead body, Elaine said. Aunt Charlotte and I looked up. *Pun intended,* Elaine added. Elaine occupied herself on the far side of the studio, examining my silver tint photographs of women half-submerged in water and sand. Elaine had never interested herself in my sculpture, only in the photography. She preferred the flat to the three-dimensional. She thought it was more cerebral, less sensual. I wondered.

I covered the clay with wet towels. Aunt Charlotte, of course, had disappeared. *What is this?* I said. *Each person gets a five-minute visit?*

Not exactly, Elaine said. *That one was much longer.*

Well then what is this? I said, looking around. *Will someone please explain to me what's going on?*

I'm the only one here, Elaine said. *You'll have to address me.*

Undress you?

You'll have to talk to me about it, she said.

So explain.

Well, it's kind of like hockey, Elaine said.

Hockney? As in the Brit-born L.A. painter David Hockney?

As in ice hockey, Elaine said. *Field hockey. As in an aggressive, physical, contact sport where you can butt in, and knock the other person out of their position.*

It's very disconcerting. Not like breakfast.

We were all working together at breakfast. It was balanced. Now we're on our own. You know. Ego sets in. We want time alone with you. We want things to happen, or in this case, not to happen. Or more precisely, if they've already happened, we want them not to happen again.

I'm flattered, I said, *but it's very disturbing.*

We'll try not to do it. We're all a little anxious, impatient. It's been awhile. We're sorry. So how are you?

I smiled at her. I had to admit, there was no one like Elaine. A lot of people thought so. She had a sort of charm, a sort of charisma in her dry humor, her complexity, her moodiness, her inner torment. She was like a female James Dean. She was tender, ironic, compassionate, restrained. She hurt, and no one could get to the bottom of what was hurting her. And no one did.

Eventually it killed her.

Suddenly it occurred to me that the focus was always on my own self-destructiveness, whether it be my failure to commit, my peripatetic lifestyle, my multiple sexual partners, my lack of financial security. And yet, these were all people who had died young—and so, perhaps, by definition, were self-destructive. On the other hand, from what they told me, I was going to live. Perhaps I wasn't so self destructive after all.

I'm fine, I said. *But Joshua ran away, you know.* Joshua was Elaine's son. I had more or less raised him from his birth to the age of two. That was after she'd left Allan and before she left me for Naomi, or Barbara, or whomever it was she left me for.

He's twenty-four, Elaine said. *A young man of twenty-four can hardly been said to have run away.*

Allan doesn't know where Joshua is.

He's looking for himself, Elaine said. *Young men in their twenties do that all the time.*

I think he's looking for you. But where?

Somewhere in Santa Barbara. Tell Allan not to worry.

Why don't you tell him?

I don't speak to Allan, Elaine said. *You speak to him often enough.*

What do you mean I speak to Allan a lot?

You see him a lot, don't you? Elaine said. *You go out on dates, maybe you even sleep with him.*

I've never slept with him, I said, in the most morally indignant tone I could muster.

Why not? He always liked you. You always liked him. He's your type—thin, handsome, funny.

I shrugged. How could I explain to her that when I was a teenager he was always in the way, and now I felt guilty?

Because he was my husband? Elaine said.

I nodded.

He's not my husband now. He's been married three times. I've been dead for ten years.

I had to agree that this was true. *But he was your husband,* I said. *That's how I met him.*

I got over him. It happens.

I smiled. Of course it had never happened to me. I had never gotten over losing anyone. I wondered why. I thought it might be because when I felt loss, I ran away, so I never got closure. The day before my mother died I refused to go to the hospital. I hadn't seen Aunt Charlotte or Andrew for years before they died. I didn't go to Elaine's funeral. I never let myself feel the grief of losing them. I never let them go. Instead I held on, rehearsing the old injustices against me: I wasn't my mother's favorite, Aunt Charlotte didn't take me away to live with her, Elaine didn't choose me, Andrew didn't choose me. Even now, when I had the chance, I still didn't confront them. I still didn't work things through. A wound has to close before it can heal. Of course, they felt free to confront me with their old wounds. They were dead. What did they have to lose?

You always think if you make yourself unhappy enough, you'll be paying proper respect for the dead, Elaine said. *Well, that's not respect.* Then she added: *No one expects you to be unhappy the rest of your life to mourn us.*

Of course that was not entirely true. At the time, my junior high school history teacher had said to me: *What are you so happy about?*

Your mother just died. I got the distinct impression he thought I was insulting her memory and I should be unhappy the rest of my life—or for a long time, anyway. Once I'd gotten into the habit, it became difficult to get out again.

It hurt me that after I left you, you went back to men, Elaine was saying.

I didn't go back to men. I got involved with William.

Elaine shrugged. *Same difference.*

When Elaine wrote me a letter and told me about her mastectomy, I was at the Fine Arts Work Center, with William. I phoned her and offered to come home to California and take care of her, but she said no, I was an independent spirit, and she had people to take care of her. At that time it was Barbara.

A year later when I was in Los Angeles, Elaine came to see me at my stepmother's house. Elaine and I sat in the den by the fireplace. She warmed her hands and told me I looked well. I told her to come back to me. I told her I would take care of her. But she couldn't leave Barbara. Barbara had her on a special diet. She needed Barbara. We slept together that night, by the fire, with my stepmother and her new husband in the next room. Elaine hadn't wanted to have sex with anyone since her mastectomy. She said I was the only one who had made her feel attractive. She said I was a very woman-oriented woman. At the time I did not know what she meant.

When I called her again her cancer had returned. She had developed a tumor and it was lying against her spine. She had been in the hospital and had almost died. When they let her out she weighed ninety pounds and got around with a metal walker. She and Joshua were living at her mother's house in Burbank. Barbara had left her. Naomi had stepped in, but they weren't living together.

When I went to see her, Joshua was at school; her mother was running errands. She made me a chicken sandwich and watched me eat.

Elaine went into remission for a few months. She could walk again, without assistance. The next time I saw her in Los Angeles she drove me to the movies. *Footloose.* She held my hand in the darkened movie theater. I wanted to be alone with her, but she said she couldn't, she had to stop cheating on Naomi. She had to stop cheating people.

Elaine called me the night before she died. She sounded very lucid. She said: *I'm going to die now. I love you, and I'll see you again.* She died the next morning.

Elaine had been my first love, and she had died at forty when Joshua was twelve, the way my mother had died at forty when I was twelve. It was too much like a pattern. I did not get involved with a woman for years after that, just as Andrew had not gotten involved with a woman for years after his wife died.

Sometimes I think I didn't get my ideas about love from my mom dying, I said. *Sometimes I think I got them from Rodgers and Hammerstein movies. That moment in* The King and I *when Yul Brenner puts his hand on Deborah Kerr's waist. And Hitchcock movies. That moment in* Marnie *where Sean Connery slides Tippi Hedren's robe off of her shoulders and kisses her.*

The moment of seduction, Elaine said. *You always loved that. You never wanted to be responsible. You always wanted someone to seduce you, override your doubts and hesitations and moral scruples, and plunge you headlong into sensual abandon, culminating in transcendent bliss. That was your idea of sex, transcendent bliss. Visions. Merging with the universe. Never intimacy.*

Doesn't everybody want that? Didn't you?

Elaine smirked at me.

Or sometimes I think I'm like one of Konrad Lorenz's ducklings, I said.

What? Elaine said.

Didn't you take Developmental Psychology? The duckling imprints with the first thing it sees and follows it around. I'm like that. Every time I go to a new place I fall in love with the first person I see.

As long as they're blonde, Elaine said.

I could remember the first time I saw every person I'd ever fallen in love with. It was often when I had just moved to a new place. Sandy used to tease me about it. When I went to Paris she told me I would fall in love with the first person I saw when I got off the plane.

Blonde ducks, Elaine said. *Yellow ducks, like the plastic ones you can float in the bath. Disney ducks—Donald, Daffy.*

Sitting ducks.

You're not eating, she said, pointing to the lunch my mother had made for me. *And you shouldn't be letting Aunt Charlotte model for you.*

I ate the lunch. Elaine watched me. *So why shouldn't I allow Aunt Charlotte to model for me?* I asked. *Is it contrary to the rules of your visits?*

I'm just jealous.

Aunt Charlotte's not my lover, she's my aunt, I said. *But even if she were, you're not jealous of my lovers. You're not jealous about Allan.*

Allan's a man. Allan's alive. So what about Allan? Why not have a relationship with Allan?

He's in a relationship with a caterer who has three sons. He's been married three times. He has five kids. He's—

Never mind, Elaine said. *It was just an idea. What about Stephen?*

Stephen had worked on the movie set with us when I was a teenager. We grew up in the same neighborhood in Los Angeles. Our birthdays were only a few hours apart. He was Italian. His father died the same year my mother died. He had pursued an acting career unsuccessfully, moving back and forth between Los Angeles and New York. He was earning money doing voice-overs in New York now. I often thought that Stephen was my other half, my mirror image, a male version of myself.

Stephen won't see me, I said. *He hasn't seen me in ten years.*

Go see him.

He won't show.

Try it.

I thought you wanted me to be with women.

I do, Elaine said. *But if Stephen would make you happy, you should do it.*

Elaine had never known me when I was happy. I didn't even remember being happy until my sister transferred the reel-to-reel home movies onto video tape and gave me a copy. Six hours worth. I watched every clip. They were taken in New York and Los Angeles before my mother died. 1955-1967. We danced, we played instruments, we swam, we went to California missions, we opened Christmas presents. When I saw the clip of me in the crib outside, and my sister blowing bubbles, I thought I would cry, but I didn't. She blew the bubbles into my face and I laughed. Then she reached in, lifted me out of the crib and put me on the grass. I ran around and chased the bubbles she blew. When she was playing an instrument and I was dancing with the stuffed monkey. It was pink-faced and chocolate-colored, and bigger than me. When she took it away from me I thought I would cry. But I didn't. I picked up some cymbals and crashed them together. I laughed.

What about Joshua? I said.

Joshua! He's my son! He's only twenty-four!

I didn't mean as a potential romantic partner. I mean, do you think he's okay? Allan said he seemed awfully depressed before he ran away. Sad. He never dealt with your death. He was just starting to. He always felt ill. He kept dropping out of college. He wants to go to film school. Do you think he would make a good director? I feel so bad for him. He's so sad.

He'll be all right, Elaine said. *So will you.*

It was funny, when I thought about my own grief it seemed unnecessary, pathetic, annoying, distasteful in its self-pity and resentment. But when I thought of Joshua's it seemed very understandable, sweet, very endearing. I was sure he was just as self-pitying and filled with resentment as I was. I could understand where the unstable childhood that followed the loss of his mother would have made him so unhappy, adrift, incapable of making commitments. Why couldn't I understand that in myself? Allow that in myself? I wondered if his grief seemed more understandable and attractive because he was younger, or if it was simply because his grief was not mine.

I have to go, Elaine said.

Already? You just got here.

I know, but Andrew's coming. He wants his time. He's impatient. I can't prevent him. I'm trying to warn you, because before you said it was disconcerting.

All right. As long as I'll see you again.
You'll see me again.
You didn't model for me.
We can't all be like your Aunt Charlotte.
No, we can't, can we? I thought: *I used to be like my Aunt Charlotte.*
I wanted to be like her again. I wanted the person I was in a relationship with to be like my Aunt Charlotte. I was tired of restraint. I was tired of being someone who turned her grief against herself. I was tired of choosing people who couldn't love me.

The Nun's Room

I HAD MET ANDREW hitchhiking when I was fifteen. I was staying at cabin in the mountains above Palm Springs with my best friend and her family. We were trying to get to the next town over. Andrew stopped in his Volkswagen Van. We got in the back with the two taupe greyhounds. *Carry On, Love is Coming* was playing on the radio. It didn't take long.

Andrew was gorgeous. He had a mop of blonde curls, almond-shaped green eyes set in a broad face with high cheekbones, like a Masai warrior, and this perfect swimmer's body. He looked like someone a man or woman would invent to satisfy their need for sexual beauty.

Of course, being the naive, ingenuous, idealistic, love child of the early 70s that I was, I thought that my connection to Andrew was more than mere lust; in fact, I thought it was downright cosmic. I wandered around town the next day until I saw his van go by, and then followed it to a garage where he was refinishing furniture. I thought of it as propinquity, when it was probably just good scouting skills.

We corresponded after that. The transformation of my lust into a cosmic connection flattered his vanity. Andrew had dropped out of the banking scene in Los Angeles for a simple life in the mountains, but he couldn't seem to get away from money. Like King Midas, everything he touched turned to money, and so once he started refinishing a few pieces of furniture, the word spread, and he was back in business again. Big business. He couldn't say no.

The next winter I went up into the mountains again with my best friend's family, and one afternoon I showed up at his doorstep in a blinding snowstorm, like the day I was born, the epiphany. It turned out our birthdays were a day apart. This too, fueled my thesis of a cosmic connection, which in turn, fueled his vanity. He gave me hot tea, plotted my astrological chart, and phoned a friend with a four wheel drive to take me back down the mountain to my friend's cabin. When I left he gave me a copy of *The Egyptian Book of the Dead*.

But the other worldly connection I had claimed was between us wasn't completely invented. Once, when I was in high school, I was visiting my dad at his girlfriend's house in Venice, California. The other voice in my head, the voice that was always sensible and logical, and kept me from being afraid, was suddenly telling me I had to call Andrew. I argued with myself for awhile about it, saying I was at my dad's girlfriend's house, it was long distance call, and I should wait till I got home; but the voice in my head kept saying: *Call Andrew, Call Andrew*. So I got permission from my dad's girlfriend to make a long distance call.

I knew it was you, he had said.

What happened?

Duane killed himself.

Andrew had anesthetized himself with scotch and Valium even before his lover Duane killed himself. After that it got worse. Before Duane died, I didn't know why he anesthetized himself. I didn't know why I was his only female friend. Then one day a very handsome young man in a white ruffled shirt answered the door when I knocked. The young man let me in. Andrew was in the shower. The young man went behind the kitchen counter and started washing the dishes. While he did this I sat at the dining room table and played with the silver swan salt and pepper shakers. I looked at the pictures of rabbits in doorways that Andrew's ex lover Conrad had painted and hung on the walls in gilt frames, and the collage painting of Michelangelo's *David*, overlaid with a musical score and some dried roses. I examined the swirls of burnt sienna plaster on the walls. I looked through the doorway into what Andrew called the nun's room, because it contained a narrow single bed, that only I was allowed to sleep in. The young man in the ruffled shirt asked me if I knew that Andrew had been married once.

No, I said.

When he was a banker in Los Angeles. She was very beautiful. Andrew worshipped her. She had been married before.

Then the young man told me, quite matter-of-factly and without fanfare, that when Andrew was married to her, her first husband came over to their house in the Palisades and shot her, right in front of Andrew.

He's never touched a woman since then, the young man said. He turned the water off in the kitchen sink and dried his hands. *You're the only female friend he's had since the murder.*

And that was all the young man in the ruffled shirt told me before Andrew appeared in the hallway with a towel wrapped around his waist. *Hello, beautiful,* he said. *I thought I heard your voice.* He swatted his blonde curls with his hands.

Hello, gorgeous.

So you've met Kenny? Andrew said, nodding his head toward the young man in the ruffled shirt. He bent down to pet his cat, Ramses III. Andrew was enchanted with anything Egyptian.

I've met Kenny, I told him. Kenny hung the kitchen towel up and winked at me.

Put something on, he told Andrew. *You're such an exhibitionist.*

When I turned sixteen I bought a Volkswagen from the money I had earned working in a leather store, and I went to see Andrew on my own. We talked, he gave me books to read. I wanted to sleep with him, but he left me to sleep in the nun's room.

Once, when I was in college, I came down on my spring break and stayed with him. He bought me silver jewelry and took me out to dinner with his friends. By then he had moved down the mountain to Palm Springs, where his furniture refinishing business was thriving.

Andrew's house overlooking Palm Springs was like a work of art. The outside walls leading up to the doors were covered with bronze mirror, so the reflection of the willow tree patterned the wall. The house was on a cliff, with just enough room for a pool in the front, inside the wooden fence. The inside walls were adobe and the floors cobblestone. Andrew had built in alcoves along the stairway to house his pre-Colombian and Egyptian artifacts. The shower was tiled, square, big enough to fit four, and had copper piping. The south wall was all windows looking out over the city lights. This time Andrew did take me into his bed, but he could not make love to me. I wondered then if the story the boy had told me about Andrew's murdered wife was true. Andrew told me he had drunk too much scotch and taken too much Valium, and then he fell asleep.

A few years later, when I was in graduate school and came to visit him, we went for a drive through the high desert in the moonlight. As we drove over the winding roads I got fleeting glimpses of the canyons and rocks and scrub cactus. Once he stopped short for a deer who was caught in the headlights. He extended his arm across my ribs to prevent me from lurching forward from the sudden stop. The deer was a large buck with huge heavy antlers spread out above his head like a fan. While we were waiting for the animal to come to his senses and clear the road, Andrew turned to me and said: *I love you, but I could never be in love with you.*

I know. I know you're gay.

I'm not gay.

To Find the Universe Inside You

AFTER ELAINE HAD left, I looked around the studio for Andrew and found him among the terracotta sculptures of the reclining women. Andrew put his drink down on the hip of one, and took off his shirt. He said he was hot. When he was alive Andrew rarely wore a shirt. Clothing seemed to constrain him; it was a nuisance. He got up on the modeling couch and sprawled out in a half-reclined position. It occurred to me that I should start using male models as well for my terracottas. I wheeled a new block of clay over and began.

You had a vision recently, Andrew said.

I looked up at him. *How did you know that?* I said.

He sipped his drink and smiled quizzically. He always seemed his most confident when he was displaying that awesome physical beauty of his.

Tell me, he said.

I told him there was a large terracotta pot on the floor at the edge of the doorway, with a yucca plant in it. Outside the sky was ribboned with navy and azure streaks. I was inside looking out. The floor was sandstone. The navy and azure streaks were not just sky but ocean. The doorway was up on a cliff or a hill, and there was a lot of dense foliage around. I was on the very top, but it didn't feel like there was ground underneath.

It sounds like a peak sanctuary, Andrew said. He took a sip of his scotch. *Lots of ancient cultures had sanctuaries, temples, on mountain peaks. Maybe it's Minoan. What does a doorway mean to you?*

Some place to go in or come out. A change. A passageway from one thing to the next. But what thing?

This part of your life to the next. Have you gone through this doorway?

Not yet.

When did you have this vision?

When I was having sex. I can lose a sense of who and where I am when I have sex. I can go other places. Or lose track of time.

What do you think sex is for?

To find the universe inside you.

But I knew this was only one of the reasons. I knew I used sex to seek the oblivion that I craved, the oblivion that served as a poor substitute for the comfort I needed and didn't know how to give myself. Some people used sex to find intimacy. I suspected that, in my search for transcendence and oblivion, I used sex to avoid intimacy.

Andrew said: *Life is a play of tension between polar opposites. If the string is strung too tightly, it breaks. If it is tuned too loosely, it will not play.* Then he continued: *Your art is very Minoan. And the Minoans looked like you: dark curly hair, light skin, broad shoulders, thin hips and long legs. They had your interest in sex and beauty and euphoria. Or maybe it's Celtic. Both cultures lived on cliffs above the sea. Or maybe it's not a physical place. It could simply be a place inside you.*

I'm haunted by it, I said.

You'll find it.

I smiled at him.

And the nightmare? he said. *The one you used to have?*

I described to him the dream about my mother. The landscape of rain and fire.

Close your eyes, he said. *Imagine it. Let her get out of the car.*

I closed my eyes and imagined the landscape of rain and fire, the falling debris, the people, animals and carts running in all directions. I said I'd get her out of there, but she said no, dear, she had to go. She put her hand on my arm. She took a small carry-on bag out of the back seat, kissed me on the cheek, opened the door and got out. I watched her. Some flaming debris came down from the sky and hit her, and instantly, that whole landscape went white, like white light, and I opened my eyes.

I can't do it, I said.

Yes, you can. Try it again now.

I tried it again. It happened the same way, except that, before she got out of the car, my mother told me she loved me, and put her hand to my face and told me very tenderly to take good care of myself. She raised her hands to the light, and I opened my eyes again.

I can't do it, I repeated.

You will. Give yourself time. He got up off the modeling stand and held me. He looked at the terracotta I was doing of him and touched it gently, with his fingertips. Then he held his hand up to my face and kissed me full on the lips.

When you're dead, he said, *there is no such thing as too much scotch and Valium.*

Chimpanzees and Bonobos

FTER WE MADE love, Andrew accompanied me back to the house. Sandy was there, helping my mother make dinner. Sandy took me into the bathroom with her.

Do you see them? I said.

Of course I see them, Sandy said. *What—do you think I'm blind?*

I still think we should order a pizza. I still think they might be a group hallucination that only affects interested parties.

The landlady stopped by, Sandy said. *She saw them.*

Wow. So how do they seem to you?

They are as you described them.

Really?

Sandy nodded. My mother came to the door and asked if we were all right, so we came out of the bathroom. I didn't mind; if she hadn't, Sandy would have asked about my day, and I would have had to lie about the necrophilia and incest. I know Sandy had envisioned settling unfinished business with the dead by talking, but I seemed to be settling mine like a bonobo. I had always suspected that perhaps we weren't all descended from chimpanzees, that maybe some of us, including myself, were descended from bonobos, and that's why I was peace-loving, bisexual, maternally-identified and highly sexed, and as a virtual orphan, I had trouble integrating into the community. Maybe I was a bonobo trying to live with a bunch of conflict-seeking, adrenaline-addicted, heterosexual chimpanzee-types, and that's why I had always been more sexual and less aggressive than other people.

Nevertheless, it amazed even me that I was still attached to Aunt Charlotte and attracted to Andrew after twenty years. But I guess I should have known that about myself, given the way I thought about sex and passion when I was a child.

My attitude was revealed to me when I was eleven, and my sister decided it was my turn to hear the facts of life from my mother. I was in the shower at the time. My sister came in to get something, took one look at my developing body and made up her mind. She left, and a few minutes later dragged my mother back into the steamy bathroom.

Look, she said to my mother. *You have to tell her.*

Tell me what? I said. *Tell me what?*

Let her get out of the shower at least, my mother said.

My mother and I went into my parents' room and shut the door. I'd never been in their room with the door shut. My mother got out the family health guides, something produced by *Reader's Digest,* and showed me the diagrams of male and female genitalia. She explained menstruation and heterosexual intercourse to me, the latter very perfunctorily, as if it had no emotional content. I imagine she wanted to take the shock out of it for me, but I must have been puzzled by the whole idea that passion could be managed, because I asked my mother how actors could stop themselves from going any further when they had to kiss for a movie.

I don't remember what she answered. I learned later you could control your actions, but my belief in the irrevocability of that passion persisted. Now I felt oddly vindicated in that belief. None of my strong passions for Elaine or Andrew had ever gone away. I was carrying them around with me just as surely as I was carrying around my dead relatives.

My mother was in the kitchen preparing dinner. For people who didn't need to eat, they were spending a considerable amount of time cooking and preparing food. My mother was making rigatoni with a special meatless sauce, Elaine was making a salad, Aunt Charlotte was deep frying cannoli shells, and Andrew was slicing a loaf of home made bread, arranging an antipasto plate, and pouring glasses of wine and water.

Sandy and I set the table. Everything was harmonious again, as it had been at breakfast, and I puzzled over what Elaine had tried to explain to me about when things were harmonious and when they were not. I asked her about this. She looked at me as if she were embarrassed I had brought it up in front of the others.

When you try to force things or resist things, they will be jerky, my mother said. *When you neither force nor resist things, they go smoothly.*

I nodded, pretending to understand.

There was an awkward silence. Sandy looked at me and raised an eyebrow, cocking her head to one side. We brought the glasses of wine and water, the bread and the antipasto plates to the table, and sat down. The others brought the salad and rigatoni to the table and sat down with us. During dinner they asked Sandy about her husband and her painting. Everyone smiled at each other. Maybe it was the wine, but it began to feel warm again, like home.

The Emotional Content of Pain

BEFORE MY MOTHER died, my sister and I had one of those 1950s-1960s lives that fell somewhere between a Disney animation film, and a Rodgers and Hammerstein musical. We were always happy, unless I had to do something new, in which case I was afraid; or my sister got to do something I couldn't, in which case I was hurt. When we lived in New York I loved school, Aunt Charlotte, the ocean, and the concrete tunnel with the crab mosaic at Jones Beach. When we moved to Los Angeles I loved school, the hot dry weather, the missions, the yucca plants, the built-in swimming pool, and of course the ocean.

Then my mother told us she was going to die. My sister and I were sitting at the kitchen counter, eating oatmeal cookies and drinking orange juice. My mother told us she had cancer and would live—maybe six months, maybe six years—they didn't know, but in any case, not much longer.

I remember feeling numb, like it wasn't real. But I must have known something. I must have known that if she left me then that fear of the unknown I had always felt, the fear she had always made me face, would overtake me. Because then I did one of those child things you do abruptly and afterward remember for the rest of your life with bewilderment and shame.

I don't remember my reasoning at the time. But I must have believed that if I had her there for six more years, forcing me to do the things I was afraid of, by then I would have enough experience to do it on my own. At twelve I wasn't ready. I would sink back into terror and avoidance.

So I asked my mother if she could wait to die until I was eighteen. She told me she would try. She died six months later.

My mother had had her own terrors. The difference between us was that she faced her fears, and I avoided mine. I wondered if I picked up some fears she had, when I was in the womb, and later. She was terrified when she had to drive my sister to the orthodontist. When my sister had the stomach flu my mother fainted, and fell right on my foot. Or maybe I had inherited her fear. Maybe it was in my genes, and I was born with it. Either way, it was still the anxious parents theory. I asked my mother about this at breakfast the next day. She was fixing me ricotta blintzes and no one else was around.

You've romanticized me, she said. *It's a common thing to do to dead people.*

But I was always afraid. From as early as I can remember. It didn't happen after you died.

You were afraid because you had a vivid imagination. Then, instead of facing what you're afraid of, you avoid it.

I know that, Mom.

I'm not sure you do. You avoided seeing me in the hospital before I died. You avoided dealing with your father and sister after I died. You avoided feeling grief after I died. You avoid intimacy. You avoided the pain and fear when you hurt your back. Now you simply avoid living. That's why I didn't want to leave you. I knew you wouldn't face anything without me. Remember when I told you I was going to die? You didn't seem afraid. You didn't seem hurt. You didn't cry.

I was in shock, I said.

The deer caught in the headlights.

Everyone wanted me to be sad, but I was numb, so I acted sad. When people gave me attention because I was pretending to be sad, I felt guilty. But I kept acting sad. Eventually I always felt sad. Now I want to be happy again and I don't know how. I know you want me to be happy,

I know you always wanted me to be. But I still think I don't have a right to be happy if you're dead.

Happiness is not the absence of pain.

I know that. But when I was a child that's what I learned it was. That's what it seemed to be before you died. I thought about my 1950s, baby boomer, Disney animation, Rodgers and Hammerstein childhood.

Loss of innocence, my mother said. *Granted yours was quite abrupt, but most people get over that.*

Maybe.

Pain does not equal damage.

I know that.

You don't believe it.

She was right. I didn't believe it. I believed that happiness was the absence of pain and pain equaled damage. I began to dislike dead people, their uncanny ability to say exactly what you didn't want to hear.

Maybe you were numb, my mother said. *But I wasn't there anymore to make you face what you were afraid of. You didn't do it yourself. You never faced the grief, the fear. Your whole life you've blundered through, avoiding everything you were afraid of. You can't do it anymore. You have to face your fear. You have to let the pain out.*

What if I lose control?

What if you do? Is that what you're afraid of?

People go crazy. People die of grief.

People go crazy if they avoid their feelings, if they keep their feelings in, if they turn their feelings against themselves—not if they let their feelings out.

But what if I do?

You won't. Trust me. I'm your mother.

How could I trust her, I thought. She'd left me when I was only twelve, with six months notice. Anyway, I didn't entirely believe her. I suspected fear, avoidance, and self-delusion were self-protecting mechanisms that shielded you when you really couldn't cope, and your situation really was potentially damaging.

You think you're afraid of being hurt again, my mother said, *so you keep yourself in a box. But that's not why. You're keeping your pain and grief inside. The danger of intimacy is the danger that someone will shake that box, and the pain and grief will begin to leak out.*

I tried to understand what she was saying. I remembered when I was six and the yellow jackets nest had fallen on me, I cried and came running out of the woods to her. She knelt down, brushed the bees off my pants and then pulled them down to examine the stings. She looked in my eyes. I must have been crying hysterically. She shook me then, rather hard.

Are you in pain, she said. *Are you in pain?*

I stopped crying for a moment and thought about it. I wasn't really in pain at all. I was just frightened. I told her no. She hugged me and brought me in the house to dress the wounds. Sometimes I think that was the nicest thing she ever did for me. I wonder if it taught me, later, to separate fear and pain, to ferret out the emotional content of pain. I wondered if I had that knowledge all along, that knowledge she had taught me, and I had just lost sight of it. I wondered if I could regain that knowledge.

I'm trying to understand, I said.

You will. Give it time. You have an infinite amount of time.

I do?

She nodded. She served me the ricotta blintzes, with a dollop of cream on top, a sprinkle of cinnamon over the cream, and a garnish of orange and kiwi slices around the edges.

I Must Teach Myself to Fly

THE PHONE RANG. It was Sandy. *Working early?* she said. *I phoned in a wake up call to your house but no one answered. What time is it?*

Six a.m. What's wrong. Should they be there?

I never went home, I said. *I thought it was around midnight.*

Time flies when you're with the dead relatives. Maybe you don't have to sleep if you hang around them. Maybe they have some kind of rejuvenating energy that allows you to forgo sleep. You've been up all night with your dead relatives. You're like a female Scrooge for the nineties.

Except it's not Christmas and I'm just as miserly as I was yesterday, I said.

Oh dear. So where do dead people sleep? Do they sleep? You should go home. They'll probably show up soon enough to make breakfast.

Probably.

When I got home no one was there, but I found another marzipan chocolate in a gold wrapper on my pillow. The refrigerator was stocked with eggs, bacon, waffle batter and fresh fruit. I thought I wouldn't be able to sleep, but the minute I put my head down I fell asleep and when I opened my eyes again I felt quite rested, even though only two hours had passed. My dead relatives were all standing around my bed, watching me.

How did you sleep dear? Aunt Charlotte asked.

Rice cereal? my mother asked. She had a spatula in her hand. The air smelled like coffee and bacon. My mother told Andrew she was sautéing his potatoes in a little olive oil and bacon fat, with garlic, and rosemary. Andrew said they would be perfect.

I followed them into the kitchen. I offered to help.

It's ready, dear, my mother said. When everyone was eating quietly my mother told me they would be leaving after breakfast.

But you can't leave, I said.

Why not?

We haven't done anything. We haven't gone to the beach. We haven't taken a walk. We haven't tried on clothes. We haven't gone to a movie.

We've done what we needed to do, my mother said.

But—

No buts. You have to let us go now.

Elaine and Andrew got up and took the breakfast dishes into the kitchen. They put them in the sink and began washing them. I went out onto the porch with Aunt Charlotte.

You didn't get to finish modeling for me, I said.

It's a shame, she said wistfully. She hugged me. I told Aunt Charlotte that I was afraid the last fifteen years of my life had been a waste. Aunt Charlotte patted me on the shoulder. *Now you can go back to being the way you were before. You can be happy, loving, curious, affectionate, sexual, playful, mischievous, childlike—but with the knowledge of its rightness. Now you know. That's the difference. That's what you've gained.*

I had a dream once, I said. *I taught my sister how to fly. We were over the ocean, along the coast in Santa Cruz. We were flying very low. I held her hand, and I taught her to skim the air just above the water. She laughed. She wasn't afraid. She was delighted.*

Like Peter Pan. She looked out at the ocean. *You know that recurring dream you used to have about your mother? Well, she really was in that place during the war, and afterwards. That really did happen.*

But she said she wasn't in the war.

She said she wasn't in Europe, Aunt Charlotte said.

So where was she?

That's all I can say. It happened before you were born.

So I couldn't have saved her, after all.

No, you couldn't have. She saved herself, that time.

So when I wanted to save her from cancer, I remembered the time before?

You tried to save her the first time, the earlier time.

But she had already saved herself.

And now you must save yourself the first time.

But I thought I wasn't dying.

You aren't dying. You're not alive.

So I have to start living again?

Yes. This is your anniversary. This is the day you've outlived her. So now you have to start living.

But I'm afraid.

Of what?

The unknown, anger, criticism, humiliation, rejection. I'm afraid something will happen that will be beyond my capacity to cope.

I'll tell you where we'll be. We'll only be a few feet away—on the other side. Put your hand up, feel the breeze.

I did. I couldn't feel anything.

We won't leave you, Aunt Charlotte said. *Don't be afraid.*

Aunt Charlotte and I went inside. Elaine and Andrew finished washing the dishes and we all said our goodbyes. They didn't take anything with them. Andrew winked at me, and kissed me on the cheek. Elaine pulled on my hair and said: *Goodbye, Kiddo. Be seeing you.* Aunt Charlotte cried and held me in a long, tender embrace. My mother looked me in the eyes. She squeezed my hands. They all smiled at me and turned to go. I watched them go down the walkway until they were out of sight.

Ramses V

I LEFT RIGHT AFTER the dead relatives left. I didn't know where I was going. I had no plan. I had no money. My retirement account from teaching was half annuity and half investments. I could withdraw the investments with a fifteen percent penalty. So I incurred the penalty, withdrew the money and left. It was enough money to travel for a year, if I was frugal. And I had learned to be frugal from paying off my back surgery debt and living on so little for so long. The summer was almost over, and I tried to get a leave of absence from my teaching job before I went, but they wouldn't give it to me. So I was AWOL—absent without leave. I wasn't sure if I would have my job or not when I came back. They said I might, but they couldn't guarantee it.

I bought a "round the world" ticket and flew from the Cape to Boston, changed terminals and got on a plane to Palm Springs. I was terrified, traveling with no plans, no preparation, no room reservations. But I was also numb, aloof, adrift. I suspected I was sleepwalking. I suspected I was fleeing my grief at losing them again.

But I so liked being in the air. I liked looking out the window and seeing all that space and blue and white. And I liked being in limbo. That was my favorite part.

I rented a white compact car at the Palm Springs airport, slung my overnight bag on the back seat, and drove directly to Andrew's house. It was on Araby Drive. Araby Drive was in the hills on the outskirts of town, and his house was at the very top of hill. Andrew liked views. His house in Idyllwild, the mountains above Palm Springs, where I first met him, was also at the end of a road, with a spectacular view of the mountains.

The house looked the same as I had remembered it, a cinnamon adobe on the outside, and a fence around the property. I rang the gate buzzer and waited for someone to speak to me through the intercom. I didn't know what I was going to answer. That I was an old friend of Andrew's? A previous owner? And had just come to look at the house? Would they let me in? Of course, it would be completely changed.

Once, when I was growing up in Los Angeles, I went to the house in Encino where F. Scott Fitzgerald had lived when he'd written for Hollywood. I found the address in a book of letters he had written to his daughter. The owners had been very cordial to pilgrims arriving unannounced. They showed me the little cottage where he had worked. They had preserved it; the room remained unchanged.

No one spoke to me through the intercom after I rang the gate buzzer. Instead, a quite handsome young man appeared at the gate. He wore gauzy, blousy white pants and no shirt. His blonde hair was curly and disheveled. He had large green eyes. He looked like Andrew when I first met him. Like a younger, thirty-something Andrew.

I'm Daniella, I said. *I knew a previous owner of this house, Andrew, and I was just wondering—*

I know who you are, the young man said. He opened the gate and motioned for me to come inside. The pool was still in the front yard, enclosed by the fence; and the willow tree was still there, and the bronze mirrored wall approaching the front door. When we reached the door he turned to me and said, *I'm sorry, my name is Brian. I was Andrew's last lover.*

He opened the front door and went inside. He ruffled his hair with his hand, then his chest with the same gesture. Then he went into the kitchen and poured himself a glass of spring water from a plastic bottle. He was barefoot, and leaned against the kitchen counter, with one foot resting on top of the other.

I haven't changed the house since he died, he said. *What has it been, ten years? Fifteen?*

Thirteen.

It's been awhile. I thought you'd come sooner.

I didn't think I'd come at all.

He laughed. *Look around. Feel free. My house is your house. Do you want some water?* He poured me a glass. *I'll get your bag out of the car. You're staying here, aren't you? You didn't book a room, did you?*

I don't have a plan, I said.

You can't book a room anyway. They're all full.

Why?

Didn't you know? Sinatra died. It's the biggest thing that's happened here since Sonny Bono died.

I gave him the keys to the rental car and took the glass of water from him. We smiled. I had never met Andrew's last few lovers. I had no idea how he knew me. I had no idea why he was being so kind. And it seemed to me that Sinatra should have died long before Sonny Bono, not after.

I went into the living room. The stereo was still under the window where I remembered; the pre-Colombian figures still lined the alcoves along spiral staircase up to Andrew's bedroom. The south facing view from the front room was as vast and spectacular as I remembered. I wandered into the bathroom. The dark tile and the huge shower, big enough for four people, were intact. I came back to the kitchen. Brian had brought in my bag and deposited it on the couch in the front room. He handed me my keys.

This makes out into a bed, he said. *Are you hungry?* He went into the kitchen. *I'll make you a salad of wild greens with goat cheese and pine nuts, a roasted red pepper sandwich on some toasted sour French bread, and some crab ravioli. Would you like a glass of Pinot Grigio? Or would you prefer Merlot? Was your trip long? Where did you come from?*

Cape Cod.

Well, you couldn't have been farther away, unless you'd been in Europe, of course.

Am I disturbing you?

Not at all. I was just thinking. I like company. He set the table and handed me a nori roll, filled with brown rice, carrot and scallion slices, and sesame seeds in a spicy ginger/ mustard/ soy sauce. *To munch on until we're ready,* he said. *Did you go upstairs?*

I shook my head. *This is so good,* I said.

He smiled. *Everything is good here. The pool, the view, the food, the weather, the music, the art: It's the good life. That's what he left me with.* He tilted his head to one side. I thought of Pippi Longstocking, who had been left with a house and a chest of gold coins. *Go upstairs. Look.*

The bedroom was the same: the giant wooden armoire looming over the bed, the same southern view of the city as downstairs only higher, the sandstone floor, the terracotta pot with the yucca plant inside, sitting on the ledge next to the window. I realized if I lay on the bed I would have the same view as in my vision, except without the ocean.

I lay down on the bed to try it. It was the same, except the ocean was missing—a landlocked vision. Before I could get up again, a calico cat jumped on the bed. It was plump and furry. It climbed on top of my ribs and lay down, purring. It licked my face.

Ramses V, Brian said from the doorway. *I don't know why he's being so friendly. He's usually skittish with strangers. Anyway, lunch is served.*

We ate outside on the patio. The food was exquisite, like at Angela's, my favorite restaurant in Santa Cruz. *How did you know what I would eat?* I said.

Isn't this what everyone eats?

How did you know who I was?

Andrew. He always talked about you. You were the one who got away.

Me?

He told me he met you when you were fifteen and he was in love with you from the moment he saw you. But he was with Duane then.

He wasn't in love with me. I was in love with him.

Everyone was in love with him. He looked at me consolingly. *Do you want to hear this story or not? Anyway,* he said that in the 1970s, *when you graduated from college, the time you went out to dinner and he gave you the silver jewelry—you remember?—*

I remember.

Well, he wanted to marry you then. He wanted you to live with him. He was going to have a darkroom installed and a sculpture studio built. Anyway, he decided not to try it. He said he tried to make love to you but he couldn't. His wife had been murdered; Duane had committed suicide. He was afraid if he stayed with anyone he loved they would die young and tragically. So he let you go. Then, as it turned out, it was he who was going to die next. Die young. He was only fifty, you know.

I put my hand on Brian's shoulder. *I know,* I said.

I ate my ravioli. I had no idea I was that important. I was not sure I believed it. *But no one even called me after he died,* I said.

Oh, that was my fault. When he was dying he wanted to die alone, and afterward I was hoarding him. I was selfish. I'm sorry. But I'm not anymore. I only had five years with him. I was the last. And now I have all this. He gestured toward the view. *Anyway, I was never jealous of you. He met you long before he met me, and you had stopped coming to visit.* He patted my forearm. *Try the ravioli.*

I did. It was delicious. He squeezed some lemon juice on it for me, and then dusted it with dill.

I'm sorry I didn't phone you, he repeated.

It doesn't matter. This is better. Now is better.

It is, isn't it?

After lunch we swam in the pool, then we sat in the Jacuzzi. I showered and we went into town and shopped. Brian made dinner: mussels, clams and prawns in a saffron sauce with rice. We drank a chardonnay with it. There was a flan for desert, with crystallized ginger in it. *What do you do, are you a chef?* I asked him.

I don't do anything. I just live here. He motioned around at the house.

You could be a chef.

I could be a lot of things.

And you don't want to?

No, I don't. I just want to live here. Sometimes living is enough. Being is enough—for me anyway. Not for everyone. Conrad doesn't have to work. Andrew left him a big enough percentage of the business. But he still does. He says the business would go under without him. But I think he just likes to run it.

Conrad was Andrew's first lover, and eventually his best friend. He was a painter and ran Andrew's furniture refinishing business for him.

Does he still paint pictures of rabbits in doorways? I asked.

He still paints. He shows through a gallery in town. I'll take you there tonight.

We finished our chardonnay. I looked at him. *Is that a true story?* I said.

What?

About Andrew wanting to be with me.

Of course. The truth.

Wasn't he gay?

He was just him. I'd like to think he preferred men, but I am a man. So, who knows. You were the only woman he was interested in after his wife was murdered.

How could he care about me so much, and I had no idea?

Isn't that usually the way?

Brian got up from the table, went inside the house, and came back out again with a stack of envelopes tied up with string. He handed them to me. They were opened, postmarked envelopes, with paper inside.

What's this? I asked.

The letters you wrote to Andrew.

All of them? Brian nodded. *He saved them?*

Every single one.

Did you read them?

He laughed. He patted the surface of the packet. *No,* he said. *I never read them.*

I turned them over in my hands and ruffled the edges. *People close to me have died too,* I said. *My mother, my first lover, Andrew. They died of cancer, not murder or suicide.*

Brian nodded. *It's hard to know what to do.*
Isn't it?

That night, lying on the couch facing the view of the glittering lights, the cat Ramses V huddled against my shoulder and breathing on my neck, I wondered why the people who loved you the most never told you the truth about yourself. It was always someone else, someone who cared less, someone who didn't want anything from you. I wanted it to be the other way around.

Commitment. Responsibility.

IN THE MORNING I packed my bag, drove the white rental car back to the airport and boarded a plane for Los Angeles. I flew into the Hollywood-Burbank airport, rented another white compact car, and drove to Stephen's family house, a nondescript ranch house on a cul de sac in Granada Hills. I knocked. Stephen opened the door.

I thought you were in New York, I said.

I thought you were on Cape Cod, he said.

I was just visiting.

Me too. Why didn't you call first?

You would have left.

Did you come all the way out here to see me?

I would have gone to New York for that.

We stood and stared at each other. He seemed shocked and uncomfortable at seeing me, as if he'd been caught in the act. What act, I hadn't a clue. It was his mother's house. She had never remarried after his father died. Stephen was her only son. He had an older sister, and a nephew.

It didn't look like he was going to invite me in. When I phoned him Stephen always said: *I'm on the other line long distance, can I call you back?* And then he never called back. When I went to see him he usually knew in advance, so he was never there. He always apologized afterward, and said he had wanted to sleep with me since he was thirteen, and that was the problem.

I came to talk about Elaine, I said.

I'm late for an appointment.

I just want to talk about Elaine. We both knew her. You're the only one I know besides Allan and Joshua who knew her.

I can't miss this appointment.

He jangled the car keys in his hand like he was shaking dice. *Can I ride with you?* I said.

Not really. Do you want to wait?

Not really.

So we're at an impasse. He beamed. Stephen was really quite handsome.

So what else is new?

We agreed to eat at a Mexican restaurant in one hour. I didn't think he would come, but I needed to eat, so it didn't matter. As I was finishing my calamari tostada, Stephen sat down at the table. He ordered a margarita.

What about Elaine? he said.

There were never any preliminaries with Stephen. Sometimes it was charming. And he always wanted to talk about his feelings: how he still fantasized about me, how he was reluctant about whatever wife or girlfriend he was involved with at the time, how his shrink had just asked him to read *The Drama of the Gifted Child* but of course he hadn't finished it yet.

You should have gone to Elaine's funeral, he said. He ordered the red snapper in a green chile sauce with rice and beans on the side. He made sure there was no lard in the beans. He had a choice of flour or corn tortillas. He picked corn.

I know.

Why didn't you?

I was afraid I'd lose it.

He nodded. *If you had gone you would have closure. You wouldn't need to talk about it.* He ate tortilla chips dipped in salsa. He looked at my meal. I asked him if he wanted some but he shook his head. He sipped his margarita. *So what about Elaine?*

Why didn't she stay with me?

Stay with you! You didn't stay with her! You left Los Angeles to go to college. You could have gone to UCLA.

I hated L.A. I still hate L.A.

He looked at me. The waitress delivered his snapper to the table. He put his napkin in his lap. *I think she felt guilty, if you really want to know the truth,* he said.

Guilty about what?

You hadn't been with a woman before.

Neither had she.

Oh yes she had.

Who?

Allan told me she'd been involved with her gym teacher, or her gym teacher had approached her or something. I made a face. *Are you choking?*

On the cliché.

Sorry. I guess it could have been someone else. But it had to be her gym teacher, didn't it?

She never told me.

Well you were so young. I'm sure she felt guilty about that too.

I approached her.

You were jail bait.

It was illegal anyway, age didn't matter.

Was it really? That's amazing.

I watched him eat his red snapper. He dangled a piece on his fork toward me and I leaned over and snatched it up in my mouth. He watched my reaction.

I was always jealous of you because you got to sleep with her and I didn't, he said.

Did you ask her?

Ask her what?

To sleep with her?

Of course not! She was sleeping with you and Allan and that prop guy.

She would have if you'd asked.

Really?

He watched me eat. I nodded.

I think she felt guilty about you, he said. *Especially after you went back to men. Like she'd introduced you to something you really didn't want.*

I didn't go back.

That's what it looked like. To her anyway.

Maybe I was hurt. Because she left me.

You left her. Anyway, you didn't look hurt.

How did I look?

Like you'd been coerced into something you didn't want to do, and you'd left Los Angeles to get out of it, and you went back to men.

Clichés! I approached her. She left me. I was too hurt to try it again. She knew it. She kept apologizing to me, telling me she didn't know how I put up with her for so long.

Stephen just kept shaking his head. *You don't understand,* he said. *She felt guilty she treated you badly and she suspected she coerced you into sleeping with women when you wouldn't have otherwise. Going back to men confirmed her suspicion.* He examined me eating. *So why didn't we ever sleep together?*

You don't want to.

I've always wanted to. I'm just afraid.

Of what?

I've built it up so much over the years. What if I disappoint you?

What if I disappoint you? Somehow I didn't think that was such a big deal. It seemed inevitable that with all that expectation there would be some disappointment. So what?

If we slept together, Stephen said, *I'd just want to sleep with you and you'd want a relationship, and then you'd get mad.*

How do you know I'd want a relationship?

*That's what you always want. It's written all over your face: **I want a relationship but I can't have one.***

So what if I got mad? He was right; I didn't believe I could have anything I wanted, especially a relationship.

Then we wouldn't be friends anymore, Stephen said.

We aren't friends now. You won't see me. You won't return my calls. I know why I avoid relationships.

Why?

Because they force you to look at things about yourself that you're spending all your energy and time denying. It's counter productive.

I see.

Stephen insisted on paying the bill with a credit card. After all, he was making three times more a year doing voice overs than I was at my teaching job in upstate New York. I thought about my friends who were successful at jobs and making money. What a gulf it made between us. They were jealous of me because I had always done what I wanted to, sculpt and photograph. I was jealous of them because they had enough money, they were successful, they were good at something, they could make use of the system that we all lived in, they could benefit from it.

Stephen didn't want me to come back to his mother's house; he didn't want to meet me later. He said I should come see him in New York, but that he didn't know when he'd be able to come see me on Cape Cod. The visit to L.A. had left him behind in his work, when he returned to New York he was going to have to stay there, and he was buying a house in northwest Connecticut, near a famous actress and her sculptor husband, and that was going to occupy his time.

I'm afraid of it, he said.

Why? The money?

No. I have the money.

Then why?

The commitment. The responsibility.

Tim? The Prop Guy?

A YEAR BEFORE I left Santa Cruz to teach in upstate New York, Allan, Elaine's ex husband, opened an Italian restaurant, *Angela's*, in the center of town, on the Pacific Garden Mall. I was looking through the weekly entertainment newspaper and came across a photo of him in a white apron and chef's cap, hovering over a table of diners. I phoned Sandy. *Allan's in town*, I told her.

Oh my god. How can that be?

The hell if I know.

Are you going to go see him?

The hell if I know.

I hadn't seen Allan in twenty some years, since I was sixteen, and he had left Elaine for Angela, who became his second wife and eventually, the name of his Italian restaurant. I spent a month deciding if I would drop by the restaurant and see him. Sandy kept asking me if I would. My boyfriend at the time, Wesley, kept asking me if I would.

Wesley had two daughters, aged eight and eleven, who started tying their athletic shoes like mine after I'd been going out with him for only a month. When I explained to them that it wasn't a fashion statement, it was a safeguard against tripping over my laces, the eight year old said it was too late to change back, her whole 3rd grade class was doing it.

Eventually I went to the restaurant. Allan was standing by the espresso maker. He looked the same except that his brown curly hair was shorter, his blue eyes sharper, and he dressed in designer suits. He laughed out loud when he saw me. *It's been twenty years and you look exactly the same,* he said.

So do you.

Do I?

He sat me down in a table by the wine rack, served me cappuccino and focaccia bread, and pulled up a chair, wiping his hands on a white linen napkin.

Wow, he said. *What are you doing here?*

I live here. What are you doing here?

I moved here to be closer to my parents. His parents lived in San José. His third wife, Rachel was divorcing him. They had two babies, a six-month-old and an 18-month-old. He had two teenage daughters in Brentwood from his second wife Angela, and Joshua from his first marriage to Elaine.

He said he felt beleaguered. So many wives, so many children. After Elaine had died of cancer Joshua went back to live with him, but Angela didn't like Josh because he reminded her of Elaine. Allan quit the movie business and stayed in Brentwood, selling Mercedes and Jaguars. Then he divorced Angela, married Rachel, and moved to Santa Cruz.

Rachel's furious, Allan said. *She wants a cut of the business. She came in yesterday and stole the cookbooks. She said it was her idea, her design, her decor, her menus, her everything.*

I looked around. The restaurant was tasteful. White walls with blonde wood accents, white tablecloths with blonde wood chairs. Tiger lily centerpieces, rotating art exhibits on the walls. A few angels here and there, Raphael's and otherwise.

Was it? I said.

Allan shrugged. *Rachel says I turned Elaine into a lesbian.*

You. I laughed. *I turned her into a lesbian.*

You slept with Elaine?

You didn't know? He shook his head. I had always wondered if he'd known. His humor was so dry and full of innuendo, I thought he'd known.

Did you know about Tim? I said. Tim was the prop guy.

You slept with Tim?

No, Elaine.

Elaine slept with Tim? The prop guy?

If he hadn't started laughing I would have felt terrible. It suddenly occurred to me that even though Allan had left Elaine it might hurt him to know these things.

I'm sorry, I said. *I shouldn't have told you.*

No. I'm glad. He reached across the table and grabbed my wrist. *I always felt guilty about Elaine. I was never interested enough in her. And then I cheated on her and left her for Angela. I'm glad you told me. Really. But Tim? The prop guy?*

I came into the restaurant about once a week after that, sometimes with Wesley, sometimes with Sandy, until Sandy moved to Boston and Wesley broke up with me when I was offered the teaching job in upstate New York. Then I started going into the restaurant by myself. Allan said he was glad I'd broken up with Wesley, that Wesley was all wrong for me.

Allan took me to his apartment. He showed me snapshots of his children, old black and whites of himself growing up in Arizona. He took me to a French restaurant where he knew the owner, and we ate French onion soup and oysters and *salade nicoise*, and drank Remy Martin and Grand Marnier. He tried to put his arm around me. He told me I shouldn't take the teaching job in upstate New York. He told me I had to see Joshua, straighten him out. Josh didn't keep in touch with Barbara or Naomi, Elaine's two lovers he had lived with. Allan's second wife Angela had never liked him. The poor kid was adrift, couldn't finish college, couldn't hold down a job; he was always sick and no one could ever figure out what was wrong with him. He was always unhappy and no one could figure out why.

I thought I knew what was wrong with him. I thought I knew why he was unhappy. I thought it was the same thing that was wrong with me. I thought it was the same reason I was unhappy.

When I met Joshua, Allan told him I had baby-sat him when he was a child. He apologized. I told him he was no trouble. Joshua was living in San Francisco then, it was before he disappeared in Santa Barbara.

After a few more months I moved to upstate New York. I never straightened Joshua out. I never slept with Allan. I never explained why. I never told him that I would have felt guilty. I never told him how important Elaine had been to me, or that he had been in the way.

I always felt bad that I never cared for Elaine enough, Allan said before I left. *Barbara didn't either. Barbara left her when she was dying. She didn't even go to the funeral. Naomi was the only one Elaine spent time with who really cared about her. But Elaine wasn't that interested in Naomi.*

After I moved to upstate New York Allan got involved with the caterer, Lynn, who had three sons. They seemed happy together. His divorce finalized. He had a melanoma removed from above his eye. He spent the his days off at his parents in San José or with his two small children in Marin, where Rachel had moved. He took his new girlfriend Lynn to New York City for a vacation and they went to Broadway shows. I saw him on my own vacations, when I would fly in to Santa Cruz from upstate New York.

I brought my sister, or Sandy, or other friends into the restaurant. The food was good there. He had the best tiramisu I'd ever tasted. When we went for breakfast I had ricotta blintzes with kiwi and strawberries. My sister raved about the poached salmon. Once he and Lynn invited me to their Christmas party at the restaurant, and sometimes I saw Joshua when he was visiting or staying with his dad between girlfriends, but I never went out with Allan after that.

I Know That Too

FTER STEPHEN LEFT me at the Mexican restaurant, I drove around Los Angeles for a while in the white rental car before I went back to the airport. I drove by my old houses in Granada Hills, Woodland Hills and Chatsworth. I drove by the shopping malls where my father had designed the interiors of Bullocks and Macy's. I drove up into the Getty Oil land where I used to go hiking. I drove by Elaine and Allan's apartment near the state university, and their house in Granada Hills where I baby-sat Joshua.

Then I returned the white rental car to the airport, flew to Monterey, rented another white compact car, and drove to Angela's restaurant on the Pacific Garden Mall in Santa Cruz.

Allan was in the kitchen talking to the chef. A waitress went behind the curtain and told him I was there. I sat down at my table by the wine racks. He brought me out a fresh mozzarella and tomato salad with basil and olive oil, and some focaccia bread.

Back for good? he said.

I wish.

You should come back for good. You don't belong out there on the east coast. It doesn't suit you.

Think so?

I do. Elaine couldn't live in northern California. She needed Los Angeles. You can't live on the east coast. You need the west coast. Different people need different things. It's not a crime. It's not admitting defeat.

Elaine moved to northern California with Barbara. It had always been a sore point with me, that she'd move with Barbara but not with me.

She tried. She was trying to please Barbara. But nothing pleased Barbara. Cappuccino?

I nodded. He made two, and sat down with me. *So,* he said, *what's new? Debt paid off? Any prospects?*

What kind of prospects?

He laughed. *The usual. Success, money, fame, marriage.*

None. What about you? Still with the new girlfriend?

Lynn? Yes. Joshua moved back in with us.

He surfaced?

Yes. You should talk to him about his mother; straighten him out. He's adrift.

I tried. He doesn't want to talk about his mother.

Try again.

We sipped our cappuccinos. Joshua came into the restaurant from the building across the street, and asked his father if he had to stack any more cases of wine or if he could take the rest of the afternoon off instead.

Do you remember Daniella? Allan said.

Joshua nodded and held out his hand. *My baby-sitter,* he said.

I shook his hand and smiled. *Daniella's going to take you for a little drive,* Allan said.

In what?

In her white compact rental car, Allan said, winking at me.

How did you know that?

Don't you always rent a white car? Isn't that some kind of superstition with you?

The things you remember.

I drove Joshua down to the cliffs above the ocean. We parked and walked the trail through the eucalyptus groves down to the beach. We sat down in the sand. Joshua scooped up handfuls and then poured them out again like an hourglass.

Your mother loved you, I said. God, it sounded so trite. *She just wasn't real expressive.*

I know.

She didn't mean to move you around so much, and in and out with so many families. She was just trying to have a relationship.

I know.

And it wasn't you her lovers didn't like, and Andrea didn't like. You just reminded them of the ex they were threatened by.

I know that.

And she didn't mean to die, I said. *She didn't mean to leave you alone.*

I know all this stuff. I've heard it a million times.

And your father loves you.

Yes.

And it's not your fault.

I know that too.

So what's your problem?

What's your *problem?*

I needed a safe, intact childhood, where someone loved me uncondi-tionally, put me first, built up my self-esteem. I never had that.

Welcome to the club.

So what do you do now? How do you get what you want? How do you feel better? Feel happy? Stop feeling sick?

I don't know what I want. I don't know how to get it. I don't know why I feel sick. I don't know why I'm unhappy.

We just reviewed all that.

But how do you get over it? Did you ever get over it?

No, I said.

See, he said.

Your father loves you.

I know. I love him. It doesn't seem to make a difference.

He doesn't know what to do for you.

I don't either.

I'm sorry I'm not much help.

It's okay. Nobody's perfect. You don't have to be perfect.

I nodded. I wondered why I never knew that.

So my mom really liked me? he said.

You were the most important thing in the world to her. And the most precious. And the most special. Really.

Really?

I nodded.

I thought maybe she didn't like me.

Why?

Not for any specific reason. Just because I was a guy, I mean.

No. She liked guys. Just not to sleep with, well, not after your dad anyway.

I drove him back to his father's restaurant. When I parked he put his hand on my shoulder and said: *Thanks for trying.* When we went inside the restaurant Joshua went up to Allan and kissed him on the cheek. *I love you, Dad.* I thought I might burst into tears, like I had when I went to Wesley's daughter's ballet recital.

Allan told Joshua he loved him too. *So did you solve the problems of the western world?* Allan said. He looked at me.

Hardly, Joshua said.

Zip It

A FEW DAYS LATER I returned the white rental car to the airport in Monterey and flew to New York City. I took a taxi to Aunt Charlotte's apartment on the Upper West Side, where my cousin Ben and his partner Jimmy now lived. The doorman was still there, and the griffins were still engraved in wood on the elevator door. My cousin Ben answered the door. He didn't recognize me.

I'm your cousin, I said. *Daniella. From California. Remember?*

He apologized and opened the door wide for me. *You should have phoned first.*

I didn't know I was coming.

We just got back from our place in the Hamptons. He called for his partner, Jimmy, who came out of the bedroom with his arms spread wide.

How could you not recognize her? Jimmy said, pointing to the piano. He gave me a big hug. *How are you, dear? We just got back from the Hamptons.*

I looked at the piano. There, among the family pictures, was a framed 8x10 of me at age seven, standing on the front lawn of our house on Long Island, in Aunt Charlotte's arms, looking up adoringly at her. I was very long limbed and very tan, had bobbed hair, and was wearing a white dress, white socks and white sneakers. Aunt Charlotte was staring at the camera. She was wearing a black Chanel suit with a gold brooch on the collar, a double string of pearls and had her blonde hair done up in a French twist.

The day you left for Los Angeles, Ben said, *Charlotte never got over it.*

We sat down in the living room. They hadn't changed the apartment at all since Charlotte lived there, except for their bedroom.

You were so special to her, Ben said, *more special even than if you'd been her own child. And we all envied you.*

And all the grown ups envied her, Jimmy said, motioning to Aunt Charlotte in the picture.

Well, your mom was her first favorite, Ben said, *and then you. They all envied Charlotte's glamorous life in the city, the life she married into. They all envied your mother, because Charlotte chose her as the one person in the family to bring into it.*

Then you left for Los Angeles, Jimmy said, *and they all swooped down like vultures trying to take your places.* He beamed.

Everyone blamed you after you left, Ben said. *You never wrote. You never called. You never came to visit. You didn't keep in touch with the family.*

I was seven, I said.

Then your mother died, and we felt guilty, Ben said. *But we took over. Aunt Charlotte needed someone to take care of her in her last illness.*

We were about to sit down to Chinese, Jimmy said. *Would you join us?*

I ate mushu chicken with them. Afterward they showed me around the apartment, all the memorabilia of Aunt Charlotte: the photographs, her jewelry, her furs, her suits, her beaded makeup cases, her perfume.

Your father wasn't very nice to her after your mother died, Ben said. *He always acted possessive towards you, like Aunt Charlotte was trying to take you away from him.*

Of course she was, Jimmy said.

She was not, Ben said. *She just thought you'd have a better life here. You would have, you know.*

I know, I said.

In the few days I spent with them, I repeated the activities I had enjoyed when I had visited them in my twenties. We went to lunch at the Algonquin, a reading at the 92nd Street Y, we went to the Thalia and Zabars. I took the cross-town bus and spent a few days in the Metropolitan, Guggenheim and Whitney, searching through the Pacific Island and Frankenthaler exhibits. All the art I loved. It made cry. It made me want to go back to work. Ben and Jimmy wanted me to stay through the weekend and see their place in the Hamptons but I told them I had overstayed my welcome and had to get back home.

Where's home? Jimmy said.

I told him I wasn't really sure.

Before I left I asked them about Aunt Charlotte's rumored affairs with women.

We don't know anything for sure, Ben said. *But everyone assumed it was going on. It was an accepted part of her social scene.*

I asked him if he knew what my mother did for the FBI.

They never discussed it. It wasn't talked about. You weren't supposed to bring it up.

Zip it, Jimmy said. *That was the prevailing attitude. You could make all sorts of innuendo about Charlotte's love life. But not a word about the FBI. Not one word.*

Every Day We Have Together

WHEN THEY PUT me in the taxi they told me to come back when I could stay longer. At the airport I took a plane to Asheville, North Carolina. I rented another white car and drove to my Aunt May's house, my mother's stepsister.

Look who's here! Aunt May shouted. The poodle barked. *You come inside! Aren't you the sweetest thing? You know how much we all love you.*

She sat me down at the kitchen table and took my overnight bag upstairs. My uncle Walt came into the kitchen, poured himself a cup of coffee, leaned against the counter and watched me while he drank it. *It's always good to see you,* he said. *You look okay. How's your sister?*

I told him my sister was fine. Aunt May came back into the kitchen, moved my uncle out of the way, opened the refrigerator and extracted a large platter covered with plastic wrap. She set it down on the table and removed the wrap. *Help yourself.* I picked up a carrot stick and ate it, then did the same to a celery stick and a radish.

There's a dip that goes with it, my uncle said.

My aunt smiled at him. *She doesn't eat the dip, dear. So how are you? Do you have a show down here? A photography assignment? I've always told your uncle Walt that you should work for the* National Geographic. *Have you been to the cemetery?*

We talked like that until bedtime. In the morning she took me to the cemetery to see my mother's grave. I cried and cried, even though I'd just seen her in person, and knew for sure she wasn't there, underground.

You know your mother's father died when she was only three, Aunt May said. *Your mother was always sad. She felt abandoned after her father died. I'm afraid she felt like she was abandoning you when she died. Is that why you never had children?*

Not exactly.

She was not the same after her father died. Your grandmother told me she beat her head against the walls and pulled out her hair for the longest time, and insisted that your grandmother produce her daddy. She thought your grandmother had sent him away. She didn't understand he was dead. When she was finally old enough to understand he was dead she blamed your grandmother. She said they'd fought that night when he drove away on his motorcycle and crashed it. When she was a teenager she asked your grandmother if your grandfather driving his motorcycle off the side of the Blue Ridge Parkway had been a suicide. Aren't they all? your grandmother said. Your grandmother was a tough woman. She survived two husbands and your mother dying before she died. She wasn't a bad woman.

No.

She just talked a lot.

Yes.

Your mother hardly talked at all.

No.

But she loved you. She felt terrible about leaving you the way her father had left her.

Yes.

I don't know what your mother did with all that grief and anger. She stopped beating her head against the wall and tearing her hair and blaming her mother by the time they moved in with us. Your mother was ten. She probably just held it inside after that.

Did your mother die, Aunt May?

No. My parents divorced. It was unusual then. Is that why you never married?

Why?

Because your mother died. I don't mean to pry.

I never met the right person.

It's hard for everyone. Your uncle Walt and I are grateful that I survived my breast cancer and he survived his heart attack. We're grateful for every day we have together.

After lunch Aunt May took me to her father's stone house where I had spent my summers when we lived on Long Island. She took me to the acres of corn and tobacco land that my great grandparents owned between Weaverville and the Blue Ridge Parkway. I looked with awe at all the wet green.

Your mother dried up in Los Angeles, Aunt May said. *It really was a desert for her, no matter how much they had watered and planted it. Leaving all her family and friends. The only thing she had left was your father and you girls. I'm surprised she lasted five years.*

Did my mother ever tell you what she did for the FBI?

Your mother worked for the FBI? She took my chin in her hand. *You're starting to look just like her. It's uncanny. Growing up you always resembled your father. But now—things are changing.*

Circle of Engagement

FTER A FEW more days in Asheville I flew back to Cape Cod. I thought I would go back to my sculpture refreshed—after all, I knew a lot more about my dead relatives and how they had felt about me. I had more information, a better perspective. But when I tried I couldn't seem to work. I was restless. I was still searching for something. A reason? A clue? An answer? The nightmare? The vision? A missing piece of my past? I didn't know what. But I decided to investigate the Minoans. Sure, it was arbitrary, but I was curious about what Andrew had said about them. Maybe *they* were the missing link. Maybe *they* would lead me to the truth I was searching for. Maybe in them I would find the doorway back into my work, back into my life. Maybe I would find the doorway through my fear, and out to the other side.

There were a lot of similarities between the Minoans and my vision. Their pottery was definitely the same as the pot in my vision, and after a week or two of research, I thought perhaps I was close to finding my doorway. Andrew was right; the culture expressed by the Minoans reflected my being and my state of mind: the love of beauty, the curly dark hair and fair skin, the top-down physiques: broad shoulders, slim hips, long legs. Also, the objects of the culture—the copper and lapis lazuli, the lilies and nautilus, the ibex and griffins, dolphins and scarabs, the palms and poppies—felt like coming home to me, as did their diet of figs and quince, spelt and barley, almonds and pistachios, olives and chick peas, goat cheese and fish.

The peak sanctuaries at the Minoan sites seemed to be at the proper elevation and distance from the sea, and the terrain had a hilliness and steepness similar to the place in my vision. But from what I could tell from the photographs, the foliage was too dry. I considered that if my vision came from an earlier time, perhaps the landscape would not have been so dry, since Crete, like many landscapes, had been defoliated—the trees were taken down thousands of years ago. But still, I did not have that *prise* of consciousness, that *frisson* that I was expecting. I did, however, suspect I had some link to the Minoans, or at least an affinity. Perhaps I simply wished for a link.

I thought perhaps I should travel there and see for myself. Reading about something in books was not the same as actually being in a place. But since I hurt my back, I had been afraid to travel, especially out of the country. Since I hurt my back, I had been afraid to do anything, really, except what I absolutely had to do—which was work. It was as if the back injury confirmed the amorphous fear I had as a child and solidified it.

Right before the back surgery I even started sleepwalking again, something I hadn't done since I was a child. After my surgery it continued. I would wake up in the middle of the night, standing in the closet with my bedding draped over my arms. Once I even found myself downstairs, in my landlord's bonsai garden.

On the nights I didn't sleepwalk I would wake up in the morning alone, in my bed, and for a brief moment I would feel the way I did before the injury—free of the pain, dread, and terror. Then I would remember my back was injured, and the pain, dread and terror would come flooding back, like the tide at Mont St. Michel. I wanted to go to that place forever, that place between sleeping and waking, where you had no pain, dread or terror. But I didn't know how to get there. And I was afraid to travel.

Everyone around me during my back injury, surgery, and recovery thought I was brave. One of the surgeons said I had a high pain tolerance. My physical therapist said that most people gave up, stayed in bed, found someone to take care of them. I had them fooled, but I knew I was an impostor. Sure, I had gone back to work. It looked as though I was living my life. But I wasn't really. I was going through the motions, and in a very limited sphere, at that—the job, the bank, the grocery store, the gas station, the studio, Sandy's, home again. My back could flare up and all that pain could return at any moment. It often did. I felt like a caged laboratory rat who is subject to random electrical shocks. The rat eventually becomes anxious and afraid.

I was sitting in my studio on one of these days, surrounded by my books about Minoan culture and the temple at Knossos, when someone said: *Snap out of it!* I figured it was Sandy, but it wasn't, it was Elaine.

Snap out of what? I said.

This wasn't what your mother had in mind. She looked around the studio at the unfinished sculptures. *Why don't you finish these?*

I'm busy.

She wanted you to go out into the world. Not recede further into yourself.

I'm trying. I went to back to California and North Carolina. I didn't mention New York because I went upstate in the winters to teach, so I figured it didn't count as going out into the world. Work was just something I had to do.

Back is the key word here. She wanted you to go forward.

I'm planning a trip to Crete. To the sites of the ancient Minoan civilization. To the temple at Knossos.

Hogwash!

She was right. I was lying. I wasn't going to Crete. *Why don't you pose for me?* I said.

We can't all be like your Aunt Charlotte.

Andrew posed for me.

He is like your Aunt Charlotte. In a way.

What way?

He's blonde. He's beautiful.

You're blonde. You're beautiful.

She waved me away.

Why don't you sleep with me? I said.

I slept with you when I was alive.

So did Andrew, and he slept with me again.

He did?

I nodded. I thought I might have convinced her.

Why do you want to sleep with me? Elaine said. *You need someone who can reciprocate. Someone who can love you. Someone with whom you can be first.*

Can't it be you?

I'm dead.

And when you were alive?

I only liked people who were reluctant parties. That was my way of avoiding intimacy. We all have one.

And I do it by picking people like you who can't love me? Who can't put me first?

That's right.

Why do I do it?

It's familiar.

Because my mother didn't put me first?

Maybe.

Am I trying to solve that problem? I always thought we tried to solve our family problems with our lovers. For some reason I had never succeeded.

Maybe. Or maybe you're just trying to avoid intimacy and avoid admitting it at the same time. Then she left.

A few weeks later, Elaine got suspicious and came back. By then I had an even better idea. An idea that made sense. And I had even researched it. I told her I wanted to look for the nightmare and the vision. I had an idea where they both were. That would help me face my fear, wouldn't it? I was sure it was the missing link, the missing piece of information that would allow me to understand my fear and put me on a path to facing it.

Elaine wasn't so sure. She asked me to explain what I'd figured out so far. I told her that the nightmare, the landscape of rain and fire, sounded to me like the atomic bomb attacks on Hiroshima and Nagasaki at the end of World War II.

Carts? Elaine said. *In a city?*

Exactly. Animals and carts sounded like a rural area. So, then I thought: the hydrogen bomb testing in the Marshall Islands after the war.

So you want to go there?

Yes. I've gotten it into my head that to find the vision, first I have to find the nightmare.

I thought your mother was in the FBI, not the Navy. And during the war, not after.

I told Elaine my mother could have continued working for the FBI after the war. My Aunt Charlotte was in the Navy, so she could have connected her up with the people in the Navy carrying out the nuclear bomb testing in the atolls.

I told her what I thought the doorway vision was. I told her that from what I had read and had been told, the coral atolls in the Marshall Islands nuclear testing area were all flat, but there were some high volcanic peaks on nearby Kosrae and on other islands in the Carolines and Society Islands. There were lots of peak sanctuaries on these high volcanic islands. The volcanic peaks were inland, and almost inaccessible. So the sanctuaries were there.

Maybe your mom was stationed on one of the high volcanic islands in Polynesia or in the Carolines, Elaine said. *Maybe she was doing her FBI work from there. Like in the Rodgers and Hammerstein movie* South Pacific.

When we were kids, my mother put travel posters up in my and my sister's rooms. But they were always travel posters of mountains. In my sister's room she put up a poster of the Mountain in Rio de Janeiro. In my room Mont St. Michel. Sometimes I thought that was why I wanted to go to France in college. Then she put up other mountains. Mount Fuji. Mount Rainier. Some mountain in the Himalayas. The movie poster for *Lost Horizon*—a snowy, cloud covered mountain. Diamond Head on Hawaii—a green mountain. Machu Picchu in Peru. Santorini, Pompeii, Rano Rakaru on Easter Island, Mt. Arorai on Tahiti, Mt Otemanu on Bora Bora, Mt. Temehani on Raiatea. Always mountains. Always *volcanoes*.

Actually, at first it was mountains, then lost civilizations on mountains, and eventually only high island volcanoes. Because Aunt

Charlotte was an international buyer for Gimbel's, she traveled the world shopping for clothes, and always came back with exotic objects from the east, from the islands.

Elaine asked me what else I remembered in the house when I was growing up. I told her about the African-looking masks that disappeared after my mother died. Before that they were always hanging on the wall in the den. I loved those masks. My father said they bought them at some cheap Pier-One-Imports-type store in the fifties. I never believed him. Now I believed they could have come from the islands. Our home movies showed some pillows with horses from cave drawings running across the fabric covers. A present from Aunt Charlotte perhaps. Or something my mother brought back from the islands.

Elaine asked me how I was going to proceed. I thought I should station myself on Kosrae, then visit the testing sites and look for the nightmare, then return to Kosrae and the other Carolines and visit all the peak sanctuaries on the high volcanic islands to try to find my vision. Of course that would not be so easy. The passageways up onto the mountains were not really passageways. They were rivers, coming down the sides of sheer basalt cliffs. Almost impossible to ascend. Especially with my bad back. I thought it would be easier to first ask the FBI what my mother had done for them during World War II, and after.

Right, Elaine said. *Just ask them. That's a laugh. Like they'd tell you.*

Why not? There had been subcommittee hearings before Congress. The documents were all available through the Freedom of Information Act. People had written books. Made documentaries. I told her this.

Have you done your research on this? Elaine said.

What do you mean?

Like the dinosaurs and rocks when you were a kid.

Yes, I've done my research.

You've always been very thorough when you do research.

Yes.

So what did you find out about the nuclear testing.

All the horrible things we did to them that we're not admitting or taking responsibility for. She looked at me askance and I wondered if she objected to my use of the word "we." Once, when I was a college student in Paris, one night an impromptu celebration broke out on the street. I opened the window of my garret apartment on the rue Descartes and looked down at the street below, where people were singing and dancing on the roofs of parked cars. The postal worker who lived next door to me was also at his window. *What's going on?* I asked him in French. He told me it was a celebration of Liberation Day. *Liberation Day?* I said.

You saved us, the young Frenchman said.

Me?

You Americans. In World War II.

Right, Elaine said. *Horrible things they won't take responsibility for. So there must be more, more they don't want us to know. Just like Roswell. Some people say we know everything about the Roswell incident. Other people disagree. The minute you go digging around into anything the government ever did between 1940 and 1970, Roswell, the Kennedy assassination, this, and you've got a whole swarm of people descending on you.*

Elaine wanted to know about the atrocities the Americans committed in the Marshall Islands under the guise of benefiting humankind, but I told her it was too depressing to go into right then and I'd tell her later.

I don't believe you're going, Elaine said.

Why not?

You haven't left the house in two months and you want me to believe that you're going to the Pacific Islands alone?

It isn't probable, I conceded. After my back injury I gradually had reduced my circle of engagement more and more. I didn't restrict myself immediately to home, job, studio, gas station, and grocery store. First I stopped traveling to other cities and states. I stopped seeing long distance friends. I also stopped writing to and receiving letters from them. Then I lost touch with my local friends. I stopped phoning them, socializing with them. I stopped driving across town. I eventually limited myself to one gas station, one grocery store, the drive to work, the drive to the studio, the drive from my teaching job in upstate New York in the winter to Cape Cod in the summer.

That's when the dead relatives came to visit. Since they'd left, and I'd come back from my trip to California, New York and North Carolina, I'd reduced the circle of engagement even more—I was finally down to the smallest possible universe: my apartment. I had always believed in Edwin Hubble's theory of the expanding and contracting universe: that the universe expands to a maximum point, then contracts to a maximum point, then expands again. If Hubble's theory was correct, my universe had contracted down to its smallest size. It couldn't get any smaller. It was time to start expanding again.

No it isn't probable, she said.

Unless you remember my tendency to go to Paris but not the football game. Have you ever heard of Edwin Hubble's theory of the expanding and contracting universe?

What? she said.

I just smiled. This was no time to try to explain to her Edwin Hubble's theory. Or my tendency to override my fear with the grand gesture—Paris, the Pacific Islands. She shook her head. I laughed. The universe couldn't get any smaller than this. It was time to go.

PART TWO

Be Mysterious
and You Will Be Happy

Tapioca and Wild Ginger

THAT WAS HOW I ended up on Kosrae.

I keep thinking of Henri Michaux's story titled, *I Am Writing To You From Another Country*. How can I tell you about Kosrae? The ocean there was wild, but soothing. The local people had a marvelous sense of humor. Three of the local women who knew me rather well—Matatea, Totefa, and Vatua—were always talking together, pointing at me and laughing. The people often laughed and pointed; it wasn't rude or insulting. The locals had a refined sense of the absurd, and they loved mockery. They laughed, and when I said, *What is it?* They took my hand. That was what they did when you asked a question. They took your hand, and they brought you to the answer.

They are a very endearing people. I know you think I'm romanticizing the exotic now, and perhaps that's true; but think of the life we lead, how riddled it is with kitsch, trash, waste, toxins, media, lies, politics, decay; then perhaps you can understand why I preferred that life to the one I had. They were very kind to me, and welcoming. I was grateful for this. The culture felt familiar to me, the way the Minoan culture did. And like the Minoans, all the women there had the same top-down physique: broad shoulders, narrow hips. They were fleshy without being fat, the way I was. And the diet suited me: fruit, vegetables, grains, shellfish.

Kosrae was a lush, tropical, triangular shaped high island, with a volcanic peak in the center. There were three rivers on Kosrae, three natural harbors, an airport, two dive resorts, and an offshore island with an ancient stone city made from prismatic basalt, like Nan Matol on Ponape. Most people farmed and fished for a living. Hibiscus, tapioca and wild ginger grew on the islands, and they cultivated citrus: tangerines, oranges and limes—as well as bananas, taro, and coconuts. The Aquaculture center bred giant clams. Lionfish, sting rays, barracuda, groupers, and parrotfish swam in the waters around the island. There were all kinds of sharks in the waters, especially tiger sharks, white tips and hammerheads, but few attacks on people. It rained a lot, but the island was below the typhoon track, so the major storms didn't hit.

The ancient stone city dated from 1400 A.D. The prismatic basalt was blue, hexagonal, faceted and stacked like a log cabin, and some of the walls went up as high as twenty feet. Royalty had lived there. The island had a history of royalty—of the islanders influencing the nearby cultures and overthrowing abusive regimes on Ponape and Chuuk up through the 1400s.

When whaling ships arrived at Kosrae in the 1830s the population on the island was five thousand. The people had no weapons, and no boats equipped for the open ocean, only 30-ft outrigger canoes. Fifty years later, their population had dwindled to three hundred, from white diseases mostly, and the islanders had set fire to one of the whaling ships and killed the entire crew. Hawaiian missionaries converted the remaining population to Congregationalism. Traders came in the 1870s and left sunken treasure boats in the harbor, and legends about hidden treasures in the uncharted interior of the island. The Japanese came in 1914 and took over the coastal villages, moving the islanders into the interior. They left after World War II, when the Americans took the islands into "Trust," turning the trade export profits the Japanese had created into a deficit.

Jets started flying into Kosrae in the 1980s, but it didn't attract more tourism. The few people who came to the island came to dive the reefs and shipwrecks. There were other natural and unnatural phenomena on the island—the mangrove swamps, waterfalls, a seventy-foot deep and ten-foot wide gorge that was subject to flash flooding, a bird cave where swiftlets made nests out of saliva and moss, and about thirty square miles of uncharted interior—but most of the island was thought to be haunted, so the rest of it was left to the islanders.

Before white people came to the island there were seventy villages along the coast of Kosrae; when I lived there there were only four, strung around the coast clockwise from the northeast to the south, and connected by a dirt road. Each town had about two thousand people living in it.

Walung was opposite these towns, on the southwest coast. There was no road into the village, and only two ways in: by canoe up through the mangrove swamps at Utwe at high tide, or by speedboat from the Okat harbor. Only two hundred people lived in Walung.

The house I was living in was built by an American, and was called the "mansion." The house sat between the breakers and lagoon, so there was water all around, and the constant sound of waves breaking. I picked Walung because there were no roads in or out of the village, it was a tiny village, the people were uncannily friendly, the ocean seemed to be all around, and the view of the misty green peaks in the distance satisfied my melancholy. I stayed because the place felt comfortable to me, and because the islanders were kind to me. The island made me homesick, but it also assuaged my homesickness.

It was not entirely peaceful in Kosrae. There was a constant wind. It pushed you, it forced your hair into your eyes, it made you squint. It was as if there was always someone behind you, dogging you, blowing in your ear. Was I still afraid? Yes, I was always afraid. Sometimes it was about the larger things, like the possibility that I had caused my loved ones pain, or that my life had been a failure, or my choices a series of terrible mistakes. Sometimes it was about more mundane things, like getting lost or injured, or the dangers of traveling, or what would happen if my back seized up on me, or I got a bladder infection.

The difference by then was that I believed my fear came more from my memory and my imagination, and less from real danger. I believed that fear was healthy, a way to alert you to danger, but I was both oversensitive and oversensitized to it; I was the caged lab rat, exposed to random electrical shocks. I felt the fear more intensely, and I tolerated it less well than others.

So I tried to face the fear, live with the fear, instead of pushing it out of the landscape entirely. I decided that it *was* the landscape. The landscape of rain and fire.

But at the same time, facing my fear had its own reward. It gave me a feeling of exhilaration; it created an adrenaline rush of release—I felt powerful, I felt freed. Now I understood why people jumped out of airplanes and skied off mountaintops. Yet the adrenaline rush was not for me. If I had a choice, I still preferred oblivion. Nirvana.

The truth was, this trip to the islands, like my trip to Paris twenty years earlier, suited my illusion of romance. I had always wanted to leave the life I had known. As a child I dreamed I would escape the suburbs of Los Angeles by stowing away on a large cargo ship, and would end up living on a tropical island in the Pacific. I envied people like Antoine St. Exupéry and Amelia Earhart, who had vanished in their planes, never to be seen or heard from again. Of course I didn't believe they had died in a fiery crash. I imagined they landed in an exotic place—Earhart on Nicamoro, Exupéry in Arabia—and spent the remainder of their days living a secret life, a happy life, far away from that other life that they had known. I feared I was still a naive romantic, searching for oblivion, all the while pretending I was facing my fear.

I planned my trip to the nuclear testing sites, sprawled on the floor in the front room of my house, eating banana chips and drinking hibiscus tea, with the maps spread out in front of me. There weren't many maps, of course, just a handful I could get from the U.S. Geological survey, and some second or third hand, that had had military uses, and some hand drawn maps from the islanders.

I tried to plan a route through the atolls that was efficient, economical, speedy, and drew the least amount of attention to itself. Of course, it was impossible to plan the trip in the real sense of the word, because most of the atolls I wanted to visit had no hotels, taxis, car rentals, airports, or scheduled boat service. Some of them weren't even inhabited. Nevertheless, I made a list of the northern atolls I wanted to visit, hitching rides on yachts or supply boats, or taking *Air Marshall Island* flights whenever possible.

I finally stopped trying to make an order out of the arrangements, and settled for a simple list of islands and atolls. As usual I was trying to prepare for what one cannot prepare for; I was trying to ward off fear and hurt, and being blindsided. But here it really was impossible to prepare. Instead, I would have to go where I could get boat and plane rides, and stay where people allowed me. I'd see what I could see. That was as much planning as I could do. I had the names and phone numbers of various Peace Corps volunteers, mayors and ministers. They were the only source of information for boat rides and accommodations in the more remote northern atolls.

What the heck is an atoll, anyway, Elaine said. She was standing over me and the maps. I motioned for her to sit down beside me.

What are you doing here? I said.

Well you can't very well do this alone.

I thought spirits couldn't cross the water.

Elaine rolled her eyes at me. *The myths about the dead,* she said. *I could fill this house with them.*

I explained to her that an atoll was a volcano submerged in the ocean. Coral built up around the submerged rim until it came to the surface in a circle of coral islands. A high island, like the one we were on, was the inverse of an atoll: an island that was not submerged, and had a volcanic mountain peak in its center.

So these people living on the atolls, are basically living on the rim of a sunken volcano? Elaine said.

Yes.

While we had the maps spread out in front of us, and Elaine was consulting my lists, the three local women who knew me—Matatea, Totefa and Vatua—dropped by. It was very common for the locals to drop by at any time in any weather, either to bring me something, give me work, show me something, or simply to watch whatever I was doing. In this particular case they came to watch. Watching was a form of visiting there. It was a small town and there were very few visitors;

everyone in Walung already knew who I was and why I was there.

They didn't seem puzzled by the fact that Elaine had joined me. I wondered if they were unfettered like some children tend to be—who see spirits of the dead and accept them without fear; or if they were like the Tibetans, and other more spiritually evolved and less money oriented cultures, who did not always distinguish between people and spirits. On the other hand, if they'd seen her arrive on an airplane, they probably assumed she was alive.

Matatea, Totefa and Vatua ate banana chips, which they called banana copra (copra is dried coconut) sipped some hibiscus tea, and listened to us making plans. They looked at our maps. They consulted each other. Matatea left, and ten minutes later returned with a young man who called himself Larkelon. She told us Larkelon had a boat with a crew and they would take us, and that the three women were coming. Larkelon smiled. Matatea, Totefa and Vatua beamed. Elaine looked at me.

Matatea reminded me that, though I may have done extensive research about the history of nuclear testing on the Marshall Islands, I knew nothing about boats, navigation, or fish. It was true, the arts of fishing and navigating were secret and passed down as sacred knowledge. She reminded me that fish that were edible on one atoll might be poisonous on another. She reminded me that the southern atolls and the northern atolls were thousands of miles apart, and that languages and customs were different on each, histories were different on each, spiritual and haunted places were different on each, insects, bacteria and potable water were different on each.

She said that Larkelon's family was from Bikini, and had lived there before it had become a nuclear testing site, and that no one could show us the islands better than he could. Finally, Matatea said that I had an uncanny knack, no matter how well intended I might be, for doing or saying the wrong thing, and that was a dangerous trait when traveling alone in a foreign country. Elaine laughed at this. *You've got her number,* she said. Then we agreed to go with them.

Dancing Summer

W E LEFT ON our trip two days later. Three young men, including Larkelon, formed the crew of the boat. I overheard Larkelon saying something to Matatea about me. Matatea replied *Koreomel*. I found out later from Matatea that *Koreomel* means *sea spirit*. It also means *ecology*.

I watched them manage the boat. I envied the confidence of youth, and I was somewhat nostalgic for it. They were strong, handsome, young, silent, and kind, like the hero in a 1940s American film noir. (I know, I'm romanticizing the exotic again). When they were not handling ropes or packages or fishnets or shouting to each other and laughing, they liked to look up at the sky and down at the water, then up at the sky and down at the water, up at they sky and down at the water, back and forth, back and forth, until it looked like a dance. I asked Matatea about this.

She asked me to imagine that the boat did not move. She said imagine that the water moved, and the sky moved, but the boat did not move. She said when they did that dance, as I called it, they were watching the water and sky move around the boat.

Larkelon did tell me what they were looking for in the water. There was a whole science of wave swells, strong swells from the south and east, weak ones from the north and west. I had read about this. He pointed out to me the main waves, and backwash waves coming back from the atolls, coming in waves and going out waves, and there were places where the waves crossed each other. He showed me the entire ocean of interlocking waves, mapped out in Larkelon's head. That was how they knew where they were.

One night I touched Larkelon's arm, under his tattoo of leaping dolphins. He asked me what my favorite fish might be. I told him that it might be Mahi Mahi. That night we had it for dinner. He winked at me.

Taongi Atoll was covered with birds. We came through the channel at high tide; Larkelon said that at low tide the water rushed out over the coral like a waterfall. On Taka Atoll the soil was black and covered with red-footed boobies, and noddy terns nesting in the Pisonia trees. We sat on the beach at lagoon side until sunset, where suddenly sheets of turtles started began to climb out of the water.

Don't move, Larkelon said. Matatea, Totefa and Vatua started laughing. The turtles scrambled past us, into the jungle behind our backs. Some of the turtles cantilevered right over my legs and hands. Larkelon smiled at this, and nodded to me. By nightfall the turtles had all scrambled back into the water. When the last turtle had slapped its way into the water, Larkelon told us we could stand up.

What was that about? Elaine said.

They laid their eggs, Matatea told us.

On Jemo Island there were more red-footed boobies, noddies, and white terns. Larkelon showed us papayas growing wild, and pointed out an array of mosses and lichens that didn't grow on the other islands. Matatea told us that, before white people came, Jemo Island was a turtle sanctuary, and that Taongi, and Bikar Atolls had always been considered bird and turtle reserves by the Marshall Islanders.

At Mejit Island we had a rough landing, because there is no lagoon. Larkelon led us to California Beach on the north west side of the island, where Totefa took Elaine snorkeling. While we watched them bob in the choppy water, we ate the local tuna and lobster, and rested on pandanus mats.

Wotho Atoll only had one hundred inhabitants on its eighteen islets. Larkelon said that the Marshall Islands were the last paradise, and Wotho was the most beautiful atoll in it. We sat on a white sand beach there and ate giant clams from the lagoon. At sunset, Larkelon pointed out the sharktooth-shaped cloud to the north, and said it would be fair at midnight. Before we left, the islanders took us into the interior and showed us a 150-pound taro they had grown. Larkelon told me later that people on Wotho attained status by the size of their taro.

In the morning Matatea told us we had seen the best of island life before white people came, and we were now heading for atolls of Rongelap, Rongerik, Bikini, and Enewetok, the atolls that had been irradiated by American nuclear testing.

Larkelon took us to Bikini Atoll first, to the islet of Bikini. The islet looked like the others had, blue water, white sand, coconut and pandanus. But Larkelon said the cesium levels in the water, plants, fish and soil were lethal. Elaine asked what radiation looked like. What it felt like. If it was palpable.

Larkelon said that it was not, except for the effects of the initial blast: the orange sky, the white powder that fell, the white hot calcium rain and mud rain. He said that on Likiep after the Castle Bravo blast, all the speckled gecko lizards that lived in the thatched pandanus roofing of the huts died and fell onto the floors there. He looked down at his feet.

Geckos are sacred, Matatea explained.

Totefa said that radiation was a form of *mangamangai atua,* the supernatural beings who dwell in space, and show themselves in heat shimmer.

Also known as gamma rays, Elaine said.

Totefa said that these forces were not harmful if they stayed where they were, but if we broke them open to us, to unleash their energy for destruction, they would harm us, as they should. She said we should know better than to unleash energy where it does not belong.

Totefa went on to say that volcanoes and earthquakes and typhoons were the ways that the earth unleashed its power, and meteors were the way that the universe brought its power to earth, and that was destructive enough.

Larkelon said the Americans cleared the islanders off the Bikini and Enewetok atolls before the testing, and off some of the immediate atolls in the predicted wind direction, but not all the nearby atolls and islands. Then the wind shifted. The blasts were much bigger than they expected them to be. These were hydrogen bombs, not atomic bombs. Thermonuclear bombs, not fission bombs. Fission bombs had limited power. Thermonuclear bombs didn't. The Mike blast on Enewetok was ten times bigger than Hiroshima. It made a three-mile wide fireball. The nearby islets within the atoll were destroyed: dead animals, stumps of vegetation, flayed fish on Enegbi, singed trees and terns on Rigili. Ten megatons. The first megaton yield thermonuclear explosion on earth. A neutron density ten million times greater than a supernova.

Larkelon said that Bikini had been cleared of its islanders since the first nuclear tests in 1946, the Crossroads tests. Rigili and Enegbi had been cleared of people during the Mike test at Enewetok in 1951, but the Castle Bravo tests at Bikini in '54 were handled differently. A fifteen megaton explosion, the largest thermonuclear device the U.S. ever tested. A four-mile diameter fireball. People were trapped in experiment bunkers well outside the expected limits of the effects. It was hot, really hot. It rained hot radioactive mud, then white rain, calcium from the coral atolls. Radioactive coral rain. The wind blew east instead of west. People on Rongelap, Ailinginae and Utirik were irradiated.

Why didn't they relocate the islanders for the Bravo tests? Elaine asked.

Larkelon said the Bikinians the Americans had relocated for the Crossroads blasts in '46 were very unhappy. They moved them to a remote southern island, hundreds of miles away, Kili island, where they had to do long hours of back-breaking farming instead of a few hours of fishing and collecting foods. The heavy surf prevented boats from landing so they couldn't receive supplies from November to March. The U.N. had intervened in the relocation, so the whole world knew about their problems. The other islanders knew how unhappy they were. If the Americans had relocated several atoll communities to do more testing in the 50s they'd have created an international uproar, and all the islanders would have protested.

So they irradiated them instead? Elaine said.

Larkelon said that the Americans knew seven hours in advance that the wind was blowing toward the atolls instead of out to sea. They ignored that. They'd had a report seven months before that the weather in the atolls was unpredictable and incomprehensible to Americans.

Better to irradiate than upset, Elaine said in her most fastidious voice. *How long did they leave them there irradiated?*

Two days, I said.

Larkelon told us that the islanders they left on the nearby atolls received half a lethal dose of radiation. The radiation "snow" got into the water system and on their food. They ate and drank it and got it on their skin and clothes. They had diarrhea, vomiting, their hair fell out, they got skin and lip burns and lesions.

Why didn't they get them out of there afterward? I said. *The minute they realized?*

Larkelon said that, despite repeated investigations and congressional subcommittee hearings on the matter, no one had ever explained why the islanders were left on the irradiated atolls for two days. There were ships outside the lagoons that could have picked them up. At a few places they came in, tested a couple of people and left. He suspected the Americans did not want to admit their guilt by removing them after the fact.

I asked Larkelon how they had lived on Bikini before the blast. He said that in the islands, anyone descending from your mother or grandmother or great grandmother was part of your family, so all the aunts and uncles were your parents, all the cousins were your brothers and sisters, all the great aunts and uncles were your grandparents. Your mother's sisters and brothers could adopt you, and then you'd have two or three or more sets of parents and could live with many of them simultaneously.

Larkelon said that, in the islands, you could sleep with anyone you wanted as an adolescent, as long as they were two cousins removed. You had complete sexual freedom as an adolescent. When you moved in with someone, that was marriage, and you had to be monogamous. When you moved out again that was divorce. But there wasn't much divorce. Each group descended from the mother lived on a strip of land that started at the lagoon side and went back in a stripe to the ocean side. So you had a little bit of everything. Mainly you fished, and you went on excursions to uninhabited islands. You played with your children.

Sounds like your kind of place, Elaine said to me.

And it's still like that now? I said, *On the inhabited islands at least?*

No, Larkelon said. *That's what it was like before the Americans came.*

Larkelon told us that since the nuclear testing a lot of islanders were displaced, either by the radiation or the American military presence. A lot of the islands were still irradiated. The fish were poisoned. The workers were grouped in the concrete and corrugated tin slums where they lived and worked for the American military bases, or grouped in cities, or on islands where the lifestyle was too different for them to feel at home. They had money from the Americans, enough to make them want things they didn't need, but not enough to restore the quality of life they had before we came. And the ones who didn't have cancer from radiation had diabetes and vitamin A deficiency from eating processed food.

And the multiple parents, the extended family from the mother, and the strip of land from lagoon side to ocean side? I asked.

Mostly gone, Larkelon said. *Except on the most remote atolls.*

I tried to imagine my mother being there, but I could not. I tried to imagine the nightmare of rain and fire and falling debris, but I knew the islanders had been removed. I tried to imagine Larkelon's extended family living here before the irradiation, each of the groups having their *watu,* their strip of land from lagoon side to ocean side. Larkelon pointed out to me how the *watus* had been arranged, and which groups had lived where, except for the western end of the islet, which had been vaporized by the Zuni blast. Even then, I could not imagine it. Larkelon reminded me it was not only the one hundred sixty-seven then-living Bikinians who had to be relocated off the atoll. I asked him who else.

All the ancestors, through the past who lived on the atoll, he said, *the nine hundred Bikinians living on Kili Island now, and all the Bikinians all the way into the future who should have lived on the atoll. They were all displaced.*

I nodded. Elaine came up and stood beside me. *A failure of the imagination,* I told her.

What? Elaine said.

A failure of the imagination, I repeated.

You mean the nuclear testing here?

But I didn't know what I meant. That was all that came to mind. So I shrugged. Elaine said that she'd once read a book by an artist who claimed that Shakespeare's plays about royalty were metaphors for the imagination, and plays like *Lear* and *Hamlet* were stories about the failure of the imagination.

Do you think that's true? she said.

It sounds true.

So this is it?

What?

Is this it? Is this your landscape of rain and fire?

No. This is someone else's.

Whose?

Larkelon's. The Marshall Islanders. Maybe even my mother's. But not my own. I was not at home. I was not facing my fear. I had left it behind, at my teaching job in upstate New York, in my studio on Cape Cod, on the back-surgeon's operating table in California, at my mother's funeral, and countless other places I could not even remember. I was running away again. Only this time instead of running inward I was running outward. I told Elaine this. I told her I thought the trip might have been a mistake.

Sometimes when you run away you run right into things, Elaine said. *Into the very thing you were running away from. It loops back in the opposite direction, and you meet it head on.*

Maybe you're right.

Anyway, there are no mistakes.

While we were standing there, feeling lost, another boat came up from the south. Larkelon said that it would be one of the American workers on Eniu, workers from California, he said, from the Lawrence Livermore Lab, who were there studying how to clean up the radiation and use potassium to stop the lethal cesium intake in the plants. They were supposed to be cleaning up the main islet, but it was Sunday, so they were not working.

Why are you here? the man from the boat said to me. *You shouldn't be here. No Americans but the workers from Eniu should be here.*

You're here, Elaine said.

What do you want to know, coming here, he said.

What don't you want us to find out? Elaine said.

Do you want to know if your mother was here? the man from the boat said. I was beginning to think he was not simply a radiation clean-up worker. How would he know about my mother?

Suddenly everyone who had been looking at their feet—Matatea, Totefa and Vatua, Larkelon and the two young men—looked up. They began to smile and nod their heads. *Bekka,* they all said, nodding and smiling to each other. *Bekka.*

What is Bekka? Elaine said, using their accent. They laughed and pointed at her.

My mother's name was Rebecca, I explained to her.

You told me her name was Virginia, Elaine said.

Virginia was her middle name. She went by it when I was growing up. But her first name was Rebecca. My father called her Becky.

Bekka, Bekka, they all said, nodding and smiling and pointing at me now. It sounded like the name of a tropical bird or one of the islets when they said it.

Well, how do they know her name? Elaine said.

I haven't the faintest idea, I told her.

The man from the boat was getting impatient. *You should leave now,* he said. *Do you know that this islet is eight times more dangerous than Eniu, the one just south of here, with the Lab workers on it?*

Mangamangai atua, Matatea said. I couldn't tell if she were simply noting the supernatural beings who dwelled in space, and showed themselves in the heat shimmer, or if she were invoking them. *Haka a raumati*. Dancing summer. Then, *Bekka, Bekka, Bekka*.

I'll walk you to your boat, the man said. He held out his arm, his palm outstretched, as if we were in a house and he was showing me to the door.

Haka a raumati, Matatea said. *Haka a raumati. Bekka, Bekka, Bekka*.

Larkelon looked at the sky. He pointed to a palm shaped cloud moving east. Heavy rain for six hours.

Do you know what's going on? Elaine asked me. I shook my head. We all followed Larkelon back to the boat.

When we got there, Larkelon and the man bowed to each other. *Your mother was wrong about something, you know,* the man said to me.

What's that?

These were not matriarchies. They were navigarchies. He and Larkelon bowed to each other again.

Why are they bowing? Elaine said.

Totefa told Elaine that Larkelon would have been both *alab in bwij* and *alab in brij* at Bikini, if they lived there now, and had never been relocated, and that his *watu* would have been the best on the islet.

Elaine asked me what she meant. *Head of lineage and head of land*, I told her.

The man said: *There's one more thing.*

Oh yeah, Elaine said, and *what's that?*

There is a place called Mt. Hiurangi, where death cannot reach. Where your ancestors are from. That is all you need to know.

This guy, Elaine said, watching him get smaller and smaller as our boat pulled away. *One minute he's the cop, the next minute the priest. Can't make up his mind.*

Americans are like that, Totefa said. *Cops and priests, cops and priests.*

From the lagoon's edge he was shouting, *Rama whit i tua*, over and over again. *Hine te ahuru, ahuru mowai. moea huru.* Then he got into his own boat and motored away.

I asked Matatea what he had been saying.

The first thing he said means light radiating at a distance. *It's a way of describing the universe. The rest are names for the unborn universe.*

The unborn universe? Elaine said.

Sheltered sleep, comfort, haven, Matatea said, *that which has not as yet unfolded.*

I went to the rear of the boat where Larkelon was standing. He was looking at the shore and waving. I looked. I thought I saw my mother there. She was smoking a cigarette, and had her arm pulled in tight against her chest. With her free arm she seemed to be waving back. Larkelon stopped waving. *Bekka, Bekka,* he whispered. I wanted to comfort him. I wanted to be comforted. With the tips of my fingers I brushed the edges of his leaping dolphin tattoo.

Mo, he said. *Jekar.*

I don't understand. I don't understand what's happening.

Einwot juon.

I don't know what that means.

We're one and the same.

I'm sorry. I don't understand.

We're all related. Kokoajiri.

I asked Matatea what he meant. She said *Kokoajiri* meant a kind of adoption when you acquire an additional set of parents.

He's adopting me as his additional set of parents?

No. He can't adopt you, you are the same.

I asked her about *Mt. Hiurangi,* where the ancestors were supposedly from. She said that all the islanders came from different places, and one couldn't generalize. She said her ancestors came from *Irihia,* the mist-enshrouded land. I asked her if that meant Machu Picchu, which was mist-enshrouded, or the Scottish Highlands, or the Milky Way, or the cosmic soup of the universe.

Matatea laughed. She said the universe was eyes only, no bodies. When I pressed her about this she laughed and shook her head. Totefa told me she meant that the universe was intelligence, energy, heat and light, but no mass. That was what they were taught.

That night on the boat, Elaine and I reconsidered my nightmare. Before we'd left for the atolls, I had thought perhaps my mother had been on one of the irradiated islands during the Bravo blasts. I had read the eyewitness accounts of the blast, but it wasn't until after listening to Larkelon describe it I realized that the blasts weren't dramatic like my dream. There was just a big boom, and the shaking, like an earthquake, then an orange sky, and this ivory snow coming down, and then they got sick. There weren't fires, the ground didn't open up. People, animals and carts weren't running in all directions. That would only happen at ground zero, if they had actually detonated a hydrogen bomb in the midst of these people. So I was at another dead end—no pun intended. I still was not sure where my nightmare could have come from. I told Elaine all this.

You might have inherited that nightmare literally, she said, *in the womb. You might have been conceived there.*

What? Conceived where?

On the irradiated atolls. Weren't you born in January of '56?

Yes. On the Epiphany.

Right. So you were conceived when, around April 6, 1955. The tests were when?

March of '54.

She probably stayed on, thirteen months or more, at least, to try to work things out. Don't you think? You must have been conceived, somewhere out there, in those islands. On those atolls.

I hadn't thought that far.

Maybe you're half islander.

Oh my god.

Everyone's always told you you weren't white. Remember how angry your mom would get in the summers in L.A. when you got so tan? You thought she was racist. She was probably afraid you were going to get skin cancer from the exposure, or question who your real father was. And the Puerto Rican designation on your financial aid form for college? How did that get there? And your Greek fiancé who kept saying you weren't white, you were Greek, Italians were Greek through the Etruscans, and Etruscans weren't white? Elaine paused. *So do you think you were born on one of the contaminated atolls?*

The contaminated atolls?

I couldn't keep up with her; I was still reeling from the idea that I might have been born in the islands, and my father might be an islander. What did that mean exactly? That this was my home? That I was an islander? Half an islander? That I had a father somewhere I didn't remember? Was that where my persistent sense of loss and longing came from? Why I always wanted to rescue people? Was that why place was so important to me? Was that why I was only happy living along a coastline? Was that why I always seemed to crave a peace and tranquility and happiness that I couldn't remember but was sure I had lost? Was that vision of the doorway, the vision I was so preoccupied with, some early memory breaking through, a memory of when I was content? A memory of what I had lost?

Well? Elaine said.

If I had been conceived on the irradiated atolls, I probably wouldn't be alive today.

So maybe you were conceived on one of the high volcanic islands. Not on the exposed atolls. Maybe you were conceived on Kosrae. Maybe that's why you chose it. Maybe that's why they let us stay in that house that they said an American owned. Maybe you were conceived in that very house.

Conceived on Kosrae? In that house?

Sure? why not? Maybe you were conceived in a high temple sanctuary, and that's why you had the doorway vision when you were having sex. Didn't Cassandra say that in Troy people had sex in the temples? Why not here? It's not that farfetched, is it?

Maybe she was right. Perhaps I had been conceived in a high temple sanctuary. Or perhaps I'd been taken to one before I was separated from my father. Or both.

No more farfetched than your coming back to visit, I said. *Where are the others?*

Nearby.

Why won't you sleep with me?

I told you. I'm dead. You need to find someone with whom you could be the favorite.

I wish I'd been the favorite with my mom.

It makes more sense that your sister was. The first born usually is.

I took it personally.

You take everything personally.

It's not even about me.

No, it's not. It's about other people—their fears, their defenses—or more mundane things like birth order.

I think everything's about me when it's not.

Grow up. You're forty.

What about Andrew? Why couldn't I be the one for him?

He was gay, for heaven's sake.

He'd been married.

The original attempt. The original denial. We all start with it.

And Aunt Charlotte? Why didn't she take me after my mom died?

You'd have to ask her that. Why haven't you? You had an opportunity to ask them all these things. Still avoiding?

She looked at me. I shrugged.

My guess is, she said, *that Aunt Charlotte felt selfish, felt you should stay with your family.*

And my dad? Why did he blame me for my mom dying?

Grief probably. Artists make annoying children. You're too curious. Too persistent. Too sensitive. The first child is an expression of love. The second makes a family, work, obligations. Anyway, your father probably wanted to be an artist himself. Didn't he paint and write poetry?

Pretty sentimental stuff.

He probably resented you.

When I was twelve?

Maybe he thought you had talent. Anyway, if you were conceived on Kosrae you may not be his biological daughter. You may have represented the islands to him, the islands that cuckolded him and killed your mother. You may have been the symbol of her death and her betrayal.

Wow. I never looked at it that way.

Me neither. I'm making this up as I go along. Anyway, he may never have realized how he'd harmed you until after he died.

Incredible. How do you think of all this? Why can't I?

Wake up. You're forty. Who am I? Cassandra? The Delphic Oracle? You can put these things together yourself.

I can?

The Moon People

After everyone else had gone below deck and had fallen asleep, I sat up on deck and looked at the stars. I thought about what Elaine had said to me. It all made sense. It could have been the missing pieces of information I had always been looking for. It was a beautifully designed, impersonal world, and it was not against me. It was part of me. It gave me peace. If I had that peace, I could face my fear. That peace was the comfort I needed. I didn't need oblivion, though I might still enjoy it, from time to time.

While I was thinking all this, Aunt Charlotte came and sat down beside me. I was glad she had come back. I told her so.

It's beautiful here, isn't it? she said.

Very.

Are you finding what you're looking for?

I think so. But I'm often terrified, I'm often uncertain. I'm often afraid I'm making a mistake or getting sidetracked.

You're not terrified now, are you darling?

No. I'm not terrified when I'm near the ocean. Or when I'm with you.

But the rest of the time?

Yes, the rest of the time.

You needn't be, she said. *We're here with you. We're just on the other side.* And she put her hand up against the air, like it was solid. Then she put her arms around me.

Can you stay with me tonight? I need someone to stay with me. I need someone to love me. Elaine won't stay with me. Elaine won't love me.

Just because someone won't stay with you doesn't mean they don't love you. She loves you in her own way. As best she can. The only way she can.

Will you stay with me?

Just tonight. And she stayed with me there, under the stars, with her arms wrapped around me. In the middle of the night I woke up and found her staring at me.

I wanted to take you home with me after your mother died, she said, *but your father wouldn't let you go. He said because I was childless I wanted to steal his children away from him. I thought it would be better not to break up the family.*

Thank you for telling me.

You should have gone to see your mother the night before she died.

I nodded. I remembered standing over the kitchen sink doing the dishes when my father and sister left. I remembered the sense of dread I had. I knew I was doing the wrong thing. I always had that sense of dread when I avoided something. I always got angry and blamed it on someone else, instead of taking the responsibility for it myself.

You should have gone to Elaine's funeral, Aunt Charlotte said. *You should have gone to your father's funeral. You don't have closure on anything.*

I guess I'm getting it now.

A wound has to close before it can heal. You never closed the wounds.

In the morning Larkelon shook me awake and pointed out a crabfinger cloud near the sun. I looked around for Aunt Charlotte but she was nowhere to be found. Larkelon told me that the breezes would remain southeast. They were mostly to the southeast. *Then why did they test here?* I said. *Didn't they know the fallout would end up here?*

He shrugged. We were at Rongerik. Larkelon showed me the fish that were toxic on Rongerik, but edible on Bikini. Larkelon said that, when the Bikinians relocated here, his relatives had eaten these fish and become sick and paralyzed. There hadn't been enough coconut or pandanus. The pandanus was poor quality and too weak to make adequate sennit rope for the boats.

At Enewetok Atoll, Larkelon took us to where Eugelab islet had been vaporized during the Mike test. Now it was a dark blue spot in the northeast corner of the otherwise pale blue lagoon. He said the water was too deep there now, and the volcano underneath was cracked. He seemed afraid. I *was* afraid, floating over a volcano with a huge crack in it, caused by a man-made nuclear blast. Larkelon took us to Runit islet, to the concrete dome there. He said they had taken all the radiated debris from the Enewetok tests—equipment, metal scraps—and stored it under that dome.

How long does it need to stay under there until it's not radioactive? Elaine said.

Fifty thousand years, Larkelon said.

How long does the concrete last? Elaine said.

Three hundred years, Larkelon said.

The area was fenced off, but the birds were making nests there. *Birds are attracted to the shimmery heat,* Totefa said. The dancing summer. The energy. The magnetism. Matatea told me that on Easter Island, on the southern tip at Orongo, on the offshore island of Moto Nui, they had the bird goddess ceremony and collected eggs in July. Matatea said *Orongonui* meant summer solstice.

Won't the birds spread the radiation everywhere? Elaine said.

Larkelon nodded. *Yes,* he said.

Yes, Matatea said. *Birds distribute things. In this case, they distribute the radiation, as does the sea, the wind, the fish, the multiplying crabs and coral.*

Larkelon said that most of the islands in the Marshalls and Eastern Carolines had been irradiated during the nuclear testing, and many of the exposed people had developed cancer. The radiation that didn't fall on the land and irradiate the coconut and breadfruit, fell in the water and irradiated the fish. So the islanders had ingested most of it. Most of the irradiated children got thyroid cancer. And most of the women. The rest got other forms of cancers. All sorts. The cancer rate there was a hundred times higher than anywhere on earth.

What's happening now? I said.

Larkelon said the islanders were getting piecemeal reparations now, a lump sum per person for each cancer, a sum that varied in amount depending on the cancer, and whether or not it was operable. For leukemia, and various throat, organ or digestive cancers, bone marrow failure, or multiple myeloma, they got 125,000. For severe mental retardation, lymphomas, severe growth retardation, meningioma, or breast cancer requiring mastectomy they got 100,000. For thyroid cancer requiring multiple surgeries, breast cancer requiring lumpectomy, colon cancer, or urinary bladder cancer, they got 75,000. For salivary gland cancer they got 50,000. For partial thyroid removals they got 37,000. For radiation sickness, beta burns, they got 12,000.

The displaced islanders had trust funds. The Bikinians had 200,000. Some atolls had school lunch programs. Some were shipped other supplies. On some islands schools and hospitals were built. On others coconut trees were replanted.

Elaine wanted to know if the islands had ever been occupied before the Americans came. Larkelon said that they had been occupied for five hundred years. *What happened then?* Elaine said.

Larkelon said that, when the Spaniards and Germans came in the 1500s, they planted coconut, and started the copra industry. That was the beginning of colonization. The missionaries came and made them Christians, but that didn't change much, except that the women started wearing dresses when they went swimming and developed skin rashes. Then the Japanese came and increased production, and variety in the crops. They introduced breadfruit, taro, bananas. It was the most productive time in the islands. Then the Americans came. Larkelon said the Americans had a 99-year lease on Kwajalein. In the 1950s the engineer in charge of measuring radiation on the islands issued a bulletin saying that now that we'd irradiated the Marshall Islanders we ought to measure the radiation levels that they ingest in their food.

So what's being done? I said.

Larkelon told us that no one had done much of anything. In the 1980s, Greenpeace had removed the Rongelap people from their atoll and relocated them because Rongelap was still too irradiated to live on. The French wanted to do nuclear testing in Polynesia and the Polynesians wanted Greenpeace to help them intervene. The U.S. Congress had an oversight hearing in '94 to begin investigating what reparations could be made to the Marshall Islands. The Bikinians had still not been allowed to return to their island.

Elaine said: *The British are going to get out of Hong Kong.* She looked at Larkelon. *I'm ashamed. You must hate us.*

Larkelon told her the islanders didn't hate everyone. They didn't blame everyone. They were homesick, and wanted their islands and their lives back, free of sickness and excessive labor, but they didn't hate everyone. Kindness was considered to be the highest virtue in the islands.

We irradiated a bunch of people who believe kindness is the greatest virtue, Elaine said.

While we were having this conversation, I noticed another small boat, similar to the one from the day before, was pulling up nearby. Two men were in it.

You're in danger, the men from this boat told me.

I heard, I said. *Yesterday. From the other guy.*

No, seriously, you're in danger.

Because I'm trying to find something out here? Look, this is personal. It has nothing to do with anyone else. These nice people are helping me. That's all. No one needs to be afraid of what I'm going to find out.

It's not what you find out that makes you dangerous, the men said. *It's what you already know.*

She doesn't know anything, Elaine said. *That's why she's here.*

The men shook their heads.

I knew it, Elaine said. *Didn't I tell you this would happen? See?*

See what? I said.

They don't believe you, Elaine said. *They think you know something. And so now you're in danger.*

Everything is personal and nothing is personal, the men said. *That doesn't mitigate the danger.*

Why is everyone talking in riddles? I said. *Am I in danger or am I dangerous? Which is it?*

Both, the men said. *You're in danger because you're considered dangerous.*

What is this? I said, *the Bermuda Triangle?*

Wrong coral reefs, Elaine said. *Wrong ocean.*

But are we in some kind of zone? I said. *Where everything's a riddle? An enigma?*

An enigma wrapped in a conundrum, Elaine said. *A mystery wrapped in an imbroglio.*

Very funny, I said.

I'm serious, Elaine said.

If you're serious, get it right, I said. *It's a mystery wrapped in an enigma, Grace Paley misquoting Winston Churchill.*

Churchill, the local women said. *Bekka, Bekka.*

What does my mother have to do with Winston Churchill for god's sake, I said.

Don't ask, the men said.

Elaine and I looked at each other.

You need to leave right now, the men said.

I don't know anything, I said.

The men rolled their eyes. One looked at his watch. *Time is now,* he said. *There's no time like the present,* the second one said. *Time's a wasting,* the third one said.

We could leave now, Larkelon said. *Let's.* He started for the boat.

On the way to the boat Larkelon said: *Tango Tango, Watea.* Matatea told me that *tango tango* meant the ocean, and that which created day and night. *Watea* was space, space that divided water so the land appeared.

Like a volcano rising out of the water, I said.

And then sinking back down under it again, Elaine said.

Do you get the feeling that everyone else here knows something that we don't? I said.

Yes, Elaine said.

Doesn't it make you feel stupid?

Yes.

Larkelon said the large serrated clouds to the north meant it would squall soon and we had to go, so we set off again.

That night on the boat I asked Matatea to tell me and Elaine more about Easter Island. I had come across it often in my research and I was curious. She said that on Easter Island there were two types of huge stone faces looking out to sea. The first kind, made of non volcanic rock, had eyes, topknots, and flat bases so they fell over. The second kind, made from the volcanic rock, had no eyes, no top-knots, and tapering pegs to stick into the soil so they didn't fall over. Matatea said that the giant stone faces along the coast on Easter Island weren't just on Easter Island. They used to be everywhere around the Polynesian Islands and Micronesian islands.

What are they for? I asked.

Matatea said they were supposed to help keep things in balance. The ones set up by the coast were supposed to keep land and sea in balance, so one wouldn't take over the other. She said the islanders believed that one of the things that had to stay balanced was the relationship between people and the earth.

I asked Matatea where she was from. She said Polynesia. I asked her to tell me about the Goddesses from her islands. The ones I had read about.

She said that the Polynesians' theology started with goddesses. The Goddess of Within was the Goddess of the Sea. The Goddess of the Without was the Goddess of the Earth. There was also a Goddess of Desire. Roo came out of the Sun Goddess' rib, not the reverse. Tahaeo and Hina—space and energy—needed to be balanced.

Hina was the daughter of the fire goddess. The goddesses told them that the earth and the people of the earth would die, that they deserved to die, but the moon and the people of the moon would live on.

Who are the people of the moon? Elaine asked. But Matatea only smiled. I asked Matatea to tell us more.

Mar meant sea and death, and *marae* meant temple, she told us. The islanders called me Dani. Matatea said that Dani could have been an island name. Anani and Tati were common island names. Ani was the name of the Goddess of Desire.

A "D" stands for two or second in many languages, Elaine said. *Deux, Duo, Dos. Maybe your name means The Second Desire. Twin Desires.*

Matatea said that Tahiti had two volcanoes that were considered sacred places of miracles, Bora Bora had one. Easter Island had three.

She said that the slope down *Rano Rakaru,* the volcano on the southwest corner of Easter Island, was where the giant eyeless faces stood up in the ground on spikes. *Rano* was the male word for moon, but the moon was female, and that *rakaru* meant to wane.

So the waning of the male moon, I said.

Something like that, Matatea said. Elaine wanted to know if volcanic rock had a special significance to the islanders. Matatea told us there was a sacred village on Ponape made from hexagonal basalt, volcanic stone from another part of the island. Elaine wanted to know if there was something sacred about volcanoes in general, but especially volcanoes submerged in the sea.

Matatea told us that in Tonga they made the same rock circles like they made at Stonehenge, with lintels, like doorways in space, only they made them out of coral. Coral doorways.

Maybe that's like your doorway vision, Elaine said. *Maybe they had doorway visions too, so they just made the doorways. Maybe everyone has doorway visions.*

Or maybe they are simply doorways from buildings that no longer exist, I said.

Elaine wanted to know if the volcanoes and the sea were simply considered to represent the basic source of life on the planet, so where they converged, on volcanic islands and atolls, this was a sacred place. She asked Matatea if this were the case.

Matatea smiled. She said that in most continents there are silicon aluminum rocks, like granite, but in the Pacific, east of Melanesia, no such rocks exist, even under water. Also in the Pacific there were deep sea trenches, from sixteen thousand to nineteen thousand feet deep. The trench below the Marianas was almost twice as deep, thirty-five thousand feet. No metals at all. Then she said that the Polynesians had 1500-year-old rongorongo boards, the talking boards with pictures on them that no one could decipher.

After Matatea left us, Elaine and I sat down to eat our coconut crab and banana. But Elaine couldn't eat. I thought she was seasick. Or homesick. But she said she wasn't. She said she felt too ashamed to eat.

The sins of the fathers, I said. *We're Americans. It follows us wherever we go.*

But we went looking for it. Most people don't. Most people stay home.

I went looking for my vision. And for my nightmare. I hadn't counted on this.

If Greenpeace asked you to help them right now, would you do it?

Elaine liked to pose these hypotheticals. Once, when I was in college, she asked me if I had to choose between being a famous artist in my lifetime but becoming unknown after my death; or being an unknown artist during my lifetime and becoming famous and having my work endure after I died, which I would choose. I said I would choose having my work endure. Who wouldn't? She said she would choose being famous in her lifetime.

I'd help them in a heartbeat, I said.

Do you think your nightmare is something that happens in the future? Like a nuclear holocaust?

No. My mother was still alive in the nightmare. She hadn't died yet.

Do you really think if you were exposed to radiation in the womb and you were going to die of cancer you would be dead by now?

Yes. My mother said I wasn't going to die. Remember?

I remember.

I like spending this time with you.

Even if I don't sleep with you?

Yes.

Why?

I was so young when we were together. I never got to be an adult with you. An adult with another adult. It's nice. I like it.

It sounds like something you could be saying to your mom, or Aunt Charlotte or Andrew.

What?

That it's nice getting to be an adult with them.

That's true. I never got to be an adult with anyone I loved. They all died first.

No wonder you never grew up. No wonder you're always alone.

Project Gabriel

A T KILI ISLAND, we waited five days before the seas were calm enough so that we could go ashore. We delivered supplies to the island on barges and picked up a shipment of copra. Matatea explained to me that we would take the copra shipment back to Kosrae, where it would be picked up by the Atkins Kroll Company of San Francisco, along with the Kosraean citrus exports of limes and tangerines.

So we're importer/exporters? I said.

More like exporter/exporters, Elaine said.

Larkelon showed me how the land on Kili had originally been divided when the original two hundred Bikinians arrived. Kili was only one sixth the size of Bikini's twenty-six islets. The Americans had built them a shore town on Kili, with houses on either side of a church. Eventually they had mapped out the small island and divided up the land, but since Kili was an island and not an atoll, there was no lagoon. They couldn't fish here with the rough water and no lagoon, and taro was much harder to grow. So, whereas on Bikini they spent two hours a day to fish and gather coconut, pandanus, arrowroot, papaya, banana, sweet potato and breadfruit, which had all grown on Bikini virtually unaided, and they had let their pigs and chickens run wild; on Kili they would have had to spend ten to fifteen hours a day to farm taro, to have the same amount of food. They were too cramped, isolated, and homesick to muster the enthusiasm to work so much harder for so much less, so instead they depended on erratic shipments of supplies from March to November for their needs. From November to March they were virtually stranded by the rough surf, unable to get the copra shipments out or supplies in, unable to fish or swim.

Now there were nine hundred people on the island. It looked like an island with a slum on it, or an American army barracks, with plywood houses, painted a beleaguered hospital beige, empty except for mattresses and televisions. Larkelon said that his Bikinians didn't love each other anymore, they weren't kind to each other anymore, because they had lost their dignity living in this way, in such cramped quarters, eating American food, with no homegrown or wild food, no fishing or swimming, no lagoon, homesick for their atoll way of life.

He said the biggest heartbreak was that the children didn't know anything else, they didn't believe that Bikini and their grandparents' happy, uncrowded life on it—where people ate crab and drank coconut milk, watched their pigs and chickens run wild and their children play—had ever existed. They thought it was a mythical land that lived only in their grandparents' imaginations.

It's a quality of life issue, Larkelon said. *If they were still living on a clean, unradiated Bikini, they'd have enough home grown and wild food. They'd have a lagoon. Even with nine hundred people, they wouldn't be crowded. They'd still be kind to each other and love each other. They wouldn't be degraded. The Americans told them they needed their atoll, and they agreed to give it up if it would benefit all mankind.*

Larkelon took my arm and brought me over to one of the small compounds of houses along the beach. I sat down on the sand. He brought me some coconut milk to drink, and a red heliconia flower, which looked like a series of overlapping funnels. He said it was for welcome. In the house behind us, someone was cooking something. It smelled good. Larkelon said it was breadfruit and coconut crab steaming. He gave me a banana to eat. Then he put down a banana leaf with some steamed breadfruit and coconut crab on it.

I don't understand, I said. *I thought they didn't eat this way anymore. I want to respect the happier life of the ancestors.*

I got up and offered to help load the boat, but Larkelon and Matatea reminded me that I had a bad back, and I couldn't. I sat down again. A few minutes later Larkelon brought a well-dressed man over to meet me. He had straight black hair and a kind face and looked Chinese or Japanese. Larkelon called him Wand, like a magic wand. But when he sat down and shook my hand he introduced himself as Wong, Mr. Tom Wong.

Pleased to meet you, I said. I thought he might know Larkelon from Kosrae, because there was a Chinese fishing company there that leased access to their waters.

When Larkelon had finished loading the boat he sat down with us. Elaine joined him. Larkelon explained to us that the men on the boats, whom I had just seen on Bikini and Enewetok, were FBI. He told me they were trying to get me out of the area because they planned to dump more radioactive waste there and they didn't want anyone around who might publicize it to the world. A woman whose mother was a former FBI agent, a woman who was currently in the islands, in search of her mother's past, was a likely person to do that. *You could witness this, live through this, and tell our story,* Larkelon said. *They will listen if you tell it, because of who your mother was.*

That's why we've been watched throughout our whole trip? Elaine said.

Exactly, Larkelon said.

Are you going to let them dump the nuclear waste? I said.

Of course not, Larkelon said. He told me that that was not what this was about. There was another group assigned to that project. *Project Gabriel.*

What is Project Gabriel? Elaine said.

Larkelon told us that Project Gabriel was this: how many nuclear devices can you detonate before the earth is so polluted the human population dies out from cancer? The major high technology governments were trying to introduce the nuclear pollution. Greenpeace was trying to stop them. And stop the nuclear waste dumping in the Pacific Islands.

Why Gabriel? Elaine asked.

The archangel, I said. Larkelon nodded.

So what is this about? Elaine said. *What is our project?*

Your being here, Larkelon said to me. *The FBI calls it Project Gauguin. We picked up the name.*

She's just trying to find out about her mother, Elaine said.

Bekka, Matatea said. She, Totefa and Vatua had joined us. They all nodded their heads, as did Larkelon.

We need your help, Larkelon said. He told us the French Government planned to resume nuclear testing in the Tuamotus. The Polynesians rioted about it and the French agreed to stop, but secretly they had decided to go ahead with the test that they had already planned.

Who are you? Elaine said.

Larkelon told us that he worked for Greenpeace. Mr. Tom Wong owned most of the black pearl farms in the Tuamotus. His business was ecologically based. He had a lot to lose if they introduced more radiation into the waters.

Mr. Tom Wong told us that the water temperature in the Pacific was rising, and this was causing the volcanic coral atolls to bleach more and more each year.

El Nino, I said.

Yes, El Nino, Mr. Tom Wong said.

He explained that this rise in temperature and concomitant bleaching of the coral was a sign of stress. This was a sign that if the damage to the environment was not reversed, the coral atolls would become more and more bleached until they died.

I feel like Alice in Wonderland, I said.

The Wild Toad's Ride, Elaine said.

More like the Mad Hatter's Tea Party.

Totefa brought everyone a banana leaf with steamed breadfruit and coconut crab, and some coconut milk to drink.

Why do you need my help? I said.

Your mother was FBI, Larkelon said. *She helped us.*

How did she help you?

Larkelon said she tried to move some of them during the Castle Bravo blast. She had a little boat. She couldn't move many of them, and couldn't move them far, so it didn't help much, because most of the northern atolls were exposed. But she brought a boatload of mothers and their children from Rongelap, Likiep and Utirik all the way to Kosrae. Larkelon believes that saved them. She saved his grandfather's life.

But if you're Bikinian, I said, *your grandfather would have been here on Kili during the Bravo blast.*

He was visiting on Rongelap, Larkelon said. He said they were sitting in 1 1/2 inches of radiation snow. The children were playing in it. Eating it. They were soaking in 175 roentgens per day, twice the lethal dose. All the water catchments were contaminated.

It was the women and children who suffered the most, Matatea said. She said it was the children who got burns, the women and children who got tumors and died ten or fifteen years later. Even now, when the islanders ingested the strontium in the crabs and the cesium in the breadfruits and coconut, it was the women and children who got tumors and died.

Bekka, Bekka, Matatea, Totefa and Vatua said. They pulled on each other's hair.

Larkelon said: *Your mother's small rescue proves the Americans knew they overexposed us. It's an admission of guilt. It would be very powerful if you, her daughter, would help us now.*

What are you going to do? I said.

Larkelon said they were going to try to interfere with the French nuclear test in the Tuamotus. Crowd the atoll islets with people and the lagoon waters with boats full of people so they couldn't detonate the explosion without knowingly irradiating them all, the way they did at Castle Bravo.

And if they do? I said.

You have to witness this, live through this, and tell our story, Larkelon said. *We have been shouting for fifty years and the testing continues. No one listens. But they will listen if you witness, and you tell it, because of who your mother was.*

I nodded. He reminded me of the Basque separatists at a café in Biarritz who had told me: *You are American. You can get us guns.*

After we ate, Larkelon introduced me to his extended family on Kili—Lebartae, Langnij, Langinmaljit, Lokwiar, Lakabwit, and the others. Even though his father and then he had remained on Kosrae, and only came to Kili for visits, he considered his relatives on Kili to be his extended family and Bikini to be his lost homeland.

After Larkelon introduced me to his family, we walked through the crowded beach front settlement to meet some of the other extended families who lived on the island, the Ijiriks, Makaolies and Rinamus, now ballooned to nine hundred people.

Your mother saved forty children, Larkelon told me. *If you multiply up the present, that means she's saved up to four hundred people by now.*

The children's descendants.

All of them, throughout the islands.

I wish she could have done more. I wish she could have stopped the testing.

Larkelon patted my shoulder. *She admitted the Americans' guilt. She took responsibility. That's a lot. Anyway, if Oppenheimer couldn't stop them, who could have?*

Larkelon told me that there have been people living in Micronesia since 1500 B.C., and Bikini was the first atoll settled. The Goddesses of the Reef told them that it was their land to live on forever. As a result, the Bikinians are unambiguous about wanting to go home. The Bikinians said that what they most loved they left behind. They said that they couldn't restore the way they used to love each other or work together until they went home.

Bikinians referred to Bikini not just as their home, but their ancestral home. They were planning to return. They said they didn't need the food there to be edible, they didn't eat local food anymore anyway; they subsisted on canned fruits, soda and salted meats. They were planning to start a dive resort to create economic independence.

Let the Americans come and dive on the warships sunk in the Baker blast. Americans loved to dive on ships, especially treasure ships and warships. Their anthem about leaving Bikini was: *No longer can I stay, it's true.* They sang it for me. It sounded like: *No longer can I stay this truth.*

I envied them their unambiguous desire to go home. In some ways my exile, unlike theirs, was a self-inflicted uprooting. I wanted to go home, but I thought I shouldn't. I felt safe at home, because I understood the landscape and the people. Home nurtured me, comforted me. But when I felt safe I retreated. I didn't go out and face my fears. Perhaps happiness was not the absence of pain. But I wanted it to be.

Twin Desires

FTER WE DROPPED off the copra shipment at Kosrae, the trip to Polynesia took three weeks by boat. Elaine said she had no idea these islands were so far apart. Larkelon said Kosrae was above the equator, and Polynesia was below. Along the way Mr. Tom Wong gave me lessons in Polynesian history and black pearl cultivation. Matatea gave me lessons in Maori astronomy and theology. Larkelon gave me lessons on wave swell navigation, astronomical navigation, the history of island boats and canoes, and forecasting the weather from the sky. Totefa taught me to play a *vivo*, which she said was the reed pipe of the ancients. Vatua tried to convince me that Amelia Earhart and Antoine de St. Exupéry had both crashed on Nikumaroro at the same time, by design, had both survived, and had both lived happily ever after, together, as lovers.

I gave Elaine lessons in French. I took her aside and said I understood she hadn't counted on this. She could just disappear somewhere along the way, or whatever dead people did to leave, if she didn't want to come with us.

Happiness is not the absence of pain, she said.

And pain does not equal damage. I was wondering why I was the last person to understand this.

Look. I'm already dead. I have nothing to lose. You keep forgetting this. You're not dead. You don't seem to understand how much this could hurt you. You don't seem to understand that this could give you cancer and kill you ten or fifteen years down the road.

It depends on which way the wind blows. This was quite literally true. *Anyway, I'm already dead. I've been living dead for thirty years. This is my chance to come alive again.*

You're not reacting.

Let me get this straight. I'm overreacting by being willing to participate in such a radical protest, but I'm underreacting to the harm it may cause me?

Once, before my back surgery, I went into the hospital to have a discogram test. It was an experimental procedure where the doctor inserted a needle into your ripped spinal disc and injected dye into it so he could see just how much the disc leaked, and therefore, just how big the rips were and where they were. I was very calm in the office, filling out forms, waiting to go into the dressing room. A nurse came out and sat down beside me. She said she didn't think I understood how painful this procedure was. *It can reproduce your original pain,* she said. *The pain from your original injury. It can hurt that bad.*

I understand that.

You're not reacting.

I understand. The discogram can reproduce my original pain.

Of course, it didn't reproduce my original pain. The doctor gave me intravenous Demerol, which made me feel completely unafraid. I watched the procedure on the monitor. The spinal discs were ripped so badly the dye just poured right out. Since the disc could not contain the dye, there was no pressure and it didn't really hurt at all. It didn't reproduce my original pain. It didn't even reproduce the pain of a mild flare up.

Nevertheless, the doctor wrote in my chart that I had a high tolerance for pain, not just in how little I felt the pain, but how little I minded it. Later, after surgery, I didn't like the morphine they gave me. It made me feel like I was drowning in mud. I wanted the intravenous Demerol again. It had made me feel like I had just had sex. But they wouldn't give me the intravenous Demerol, so I just used ice packs.

The doctors said they'd never seen anyone do without painkillers after surgery the way I had. They praised me. I bragged that I had the pain tolerance of a Martian. But Sandy said she didn't think it was good to have such a high pain tolerance. She thought it was dangerous. You could get hurt way too much. I didn't agree with her then. Now I think she was right. I always went to extremes. I either protected myself too much, withdrawing, never letting anyone in; or I protected myself too little, abandoning myself to people or situations without any restraint or caution, without protecting myself at all from the hurt they might cause me.

Elaine said: *You don't seem to understand how much this could hurt you.*

Maybe I'm still numb. Maybe I want to wake up.

Bang! Wake up, you're dead. This manner of waking yourself up does not make sense to me.

This isn't about me anymore. It's about them. They asked me to help them and I agreed. I took responsibility. I made a commitment. Isn't that what growing up is? Coming out of yourself? Focusing on others? Helping others? Moving from the personal to the political?

In a situation this extreme it sounds suicidal to me.

You were the one who was always so political.

It was the sixties. Everyone was political then. Anyway, I died. You change when you die.

It feels better to focus on other people. It feels better to give. I'm sick of me.

Altruism as a form of escape from self. You're becoming quite complex.

All the way to Polynesia, when we would come close to an island or atoll, I would find Larkelon at the rear of the boat, looking to shore. When I looked to shore where he was looking, I would see my mother, standing by the water's edge, waving with her free hand, a cigarette in the other. *Bekka, Bekka,* Larkelon would say.

One morning when the sun was particularly bright, and the water particularly aquamarine, I asked Matatea what my mother did for the FBI. She said she didn't know; all she knew was that my mother had been an art collector. She collected Pacific Island art, with *Karlat.* I wondered if this was why Aunt Charlotte continued traveling, first buying fabrics, and then eventually buying clothes for Gimbels.

Aunt Charlotte? I said.

Karlat, Matatea said. Yes. *Larkelon is named after Karlat.*

And did my mother stay on Kosrae?

Yes. Bekka dropped off the children and their mothers, then our parents hid her in the interior. Eventually Karlat came.

Aunt Charlotte came? When?

Yes, Karlat came. She had been with your mother during the test. Then Bekka dropped the children and mothers off. Then later, Karlat came.

And for how long did you hide my mother and Aunt Charlotte in the interior?

A year. Maybe two.

Was I born there?

Bekka, Bekka, she said, *Karlat, Karlat.* She was patting my head and smiling.

Where in the interior did you hide them?

It is a sacred place. Difficult to get to.

Is it high?

High?

High up, I mean.

Yes, it is high. Very high up. You can see all three harbors. You feel like you are flying.

Will you take me there when we get back to Kosrae?

We will all have to go there when we get back to Kosrae.

Was I born there? I asked again.

It is a sacred place. It is very high up, Matatea repeated. *You feel like you are flying.*

I asked Matatea why the FBI agent had said my mother was wrong, and the islands were navigarchies not matriarchies. Matatea told me that from her art collecting my mother had become very knowledgeable about the history, customs, theology and spirituality of the islands. She told the FBI how the relocations were restructuring the land disputes and turning the cultures from matriarchies into patriarchies.

Matatea said that my mother tried to get the Americans on Kili to help the islanders help themselves, not help them in a way that made them dependent and helpless. She tried to get the Americans to build the Bikinians huts in the configuration of *watus* like they had on Bikini before the Americans relocated them, with two or three pandanus-thatched wooden buildings for sleeping and cooking on the lagoon side, and the five-acre land parcel stretching from the lagoon to the ocean.

But the Americans insisted on building ten-by-ten-foot concrete rooms with tin roofs, in the configuration of an American army base, all the buildings huddled up together along the shore street, with a church and a park in the middle.

Were they navigarchies? I said.

They were both matriarchies and navigarchies, Matatea said. *Your mother understood this. The FBI does not. They think that you couldn't have a navigarchy and matriarchy together. But these islanders did.*

Twin desires, I said.

Adventures in Atomic Wonderland

L ARKELON DROPPED ME and Elaine off on one of the islets of Mururoa Atoll in the Tuamotus, where Mr. Tom Wong had one of his black pearl farms. We were instructed to wait by a white car that had a radio in it. Larkelon said he would communicate with us on the radio. I told Elaine that my father had been a radio operator in the Aleutian Islands during World War II. *Which father?* she said. Matatea had told us that in Polynesia children had birth parents and adoptive parents, called nurse parents. I wondered if the father I knew as my biological father had really been my adoptive father, my nurse father.

The atolls and high islands in Polynesia looked at first like the Micronesian atolls and islands we'd visited, but they were actually quite different. The Polynesians had guava and giant ferns growing wild in the interior of their high islands, bourao and ironwood trees, giant eels swimming in pools under waterfalls, flowering arbutus and sacred mango trees.

Vanilla was their cash crop. Many Polynesians still lived outdoors, in pandanus thatched houses lifted off the ground on split bamboo tree trunks. They had not adopted the army barracks housing with corrugated tin roofs that the Micronesians had inherited from their Japanese and American occupations. The Polynesians had been colonized by the French, and had not yet won their independence back. In school they learned French history and French language instead of Polynesian history and Polynesian language. But the blue and white flag flew on many boats, lawns, rooftops and residences, and Oscar

Temaru headed up the Independence Party that was running against the French Polynesian president Gaston Fosse in the next election.

Mr. Tom Wong said the French Polynesians would need half a million tourists per year to afford their independence, three times the tourists they had under France, and that volume of tourists would wreck the serenity. Papeete was a European city. Land on Moorea cost eight hundred thousand dollars per acre. Cars in French Polynesia cost three times what they would sell for in Europe or the United States. The nuclear testing program had brought money and jobs into the economy. But the black pearl farms were changing the local economy, providing it with a third of its jobs and income after tourism and nuclear testing. Mr. Tom Wong believed that the black pearl farms, along with an increase in tourism, might be enough to float the economy without the French. He said that colonialism was based on making the indigenous population economically dependent and stripping them of their language, culture and history. *Colonialism makes you a foreigner in your own country*, he said.

Black pearls are not black. Mr. Tom Wong's assistant took us on a tour of the sorting rooms, where the black pearls sat in shallow basins. Black pearls can be indigo blue, like squid ink, or a purplish gray, like an octopus. They can be dark chocolate brown, like a coconut skin, or a dusky, whitened brown. They can be rusty yellow, or even milky yellow. They can be green flecked with black, like malachite.

When the Weapons Division wrote up its report about the Mike tests at Enewetok Atoll, it concluded by saying: *The atomic energy proving grounds at Enewetok lie ready and waiting for man's next adventure into Atomic Wonderland.* I thought about this as Elaine and I leaned against the white car and waited. I propped the driver door open and turned the radio on so I could hear if Larkelon spoke to me. I could see boats crowding the lagoon, and imagined the people being deposited on different islets in the atoll until they were all full. I could hear shouting through megaphones but could not make out if the voices were Greenpeace, or the islanders they were helping, or the nuclear testing administrators they were trying to stop.

Elaine mumbled something that sounded like *Idiocy.* Her rage seemed to build every day. I didn't know if she was angry because of what we'd done to the islanders or if she was angry because she felt obliged to participate in a life-threatening protest when she was already dead. I asked her which it was.

I'm angry because you don't seem to understand what you're risking. You never seem to understand what you're risking.

I do understand.

I thought about how afraid I was of the unknown. But when the danger came, I became unnaturally calm. There seemed to be no way to explain this to her.

When I remarked that the blue lagoon water and the blue in the Polynesian flag of independence were the same aquamarine color, Elaine said they were not aquamarine but turquoise. I said they were aquamarine, that turquoise was a deeper, richer color, with less white in it. She was about to object when I told her that aquamarine was my mother's favorite color. She had a two-toned '56 Chevy that was half aquamarine and half slate grey. We kept that car until after my mother died. My sister learned to drive in it. We also had a Rambler that I called turquoise; my mother always told me it was not turquoise, but aquamarine. My mother rarely corrected me, except about the color of the Rambler.

I told Elaine that I had always wanted a white car, like the one we were leaning against, and that when I went home to California I always rented a white car. Elaine wanted to know if I had felt this desire before or after I had the dream about my father dropping me off at the airport in his army uniform in a white car.

Elaine said that what was beautiful about the water in those lagoons was the navy streaks she sometimes saw swirling through the aquamarine. She said it made it look like a sky in a van Gogh painting.

Not a Gauguin painting? I said. Matatea had told me that Gauguin used to walk around the town of Taravao, on the less frequented southeastern shore of Tahiti, announcing that he loved fat, vicious women. When he approached the Tahitian government on a diplomatic mission, they suspected him of being a spy. He became a famous artist only by leaving France and dedicating himself to Tahiti; he would betray himself and his art if he went back again. He died defending a Polynesian woman who had been raped with a stick. After he died everything in his house on Tahiti was removed, except for a wood carving that said: *Be mysterious and you will be happy. Love and you will be happy.*

Not a Gauguin, Elaine said, *a van Gogh.*

The megaphone noises were getting harsher and more urgent, and I could see more and more boats crowding the lagoon. Larkelon got on the radio and said it was three minutes to blast time. Elaine said she couldn't believe we were all going to just stand there and get irradiated voluntarily. *What good will it do?*

I told her I didn't know. *Should we get in the car?*

Elaine shrugged and said she thought metal absorbed radiation as badly as anything and the glass could shatter, but we got in anyway. I threw my camera bag on the back seat and hunched over the wheel. We waited. The lagoon was full of boats, and the megaphone blare was constant now. Eventually there was a low ominous rumbling noise and everything started to lurch and jerk, like in an earthquake. The sky illuminated a bright white, then orange, then it filled up with fog. The coconut trees bent back, their leaves pulled off and then incinerated. Dirt and underbrush exploded up from the ground as if it were being clawed by an invisible force.

Lightning ripped through the fog, setting fire to whatever it struck. Bananas and coconuts ignited and fell to the ground in flames. It began to rain hot water, then hot mud, then hot white calcium. Steam rose from the ground. Birds scrambled on the sand, jerking their heads and flapping their wings. Waves from the usually placid lagoon washed flayed fish up onto shore. People began to run by the black pearl farm's sorting buildings, pushing carts, pointing and screaming directions at each other. Dogs ran close to their heels. A yellow powder began to fall. Eventually a rainbow appeared in the fog over the lagoon.

I gripped the wheel. This was my fear. I was looking right at it: The fear of loss, the fear of pain, the fear of something going terribly and irrevocably wrong, so that your life is never the same again. This was the fear of my mother dying, the fear of my back injury, of not being able to take care of myself. This was my fear, palpable, bright, and explosive. I had made my fear real.

It felt better in a way—like a release. You could point to it and say: Look, this is my fear. It was not the dread I felt after my mother died, after my back surgery, the fear I could not point to or grasp. I wondered if that was why people blew each other up, gassed each other, enslaved and murdered each other, or turned it against themselves and overdosed, crashed their cars, starved themselves to death. They were making their fear real.

But at the same time it felt false, like a subterfuge, an evasion. After all, the real fear was inside, not outside. The real fear was about what might happen, what could happen, not about what did happen. Because when the present came, and you were forced to act, you often acted without fear.

I turned to Elaine to tell her I would get her out of there just as soon as it was over. We'd find Larkelon, we'd find a boat going out. But Elaine wasn't sitting in the passenger seat. My mother was.

I'll get you out of here, I'll get you out of here, I said.

I asked you to face your fears, not run headlong into suicidal danger. You've gone from one extreme to the other. Can't you ever be moderate?

But you were waving, from the different shores.

I was waving you away, motioning to you to go back. You've gone from extreme avoidance to monumental recklessness.

You did it. You exposed yourself to help them.

I was already here. I was already exposed. I was already implicated.

So was I.

My mother opened the car door and put her palm against my cheek. *I love you,* she said. Flushed with adrenaline as I was, this sounded to me like an afterthought.

I wasn't your favorite, I said.

Is that what this is about? You're going to go to extremes and come in second your whole life, because you weren't my favorite? Is it written in stone?

No, it wasn't written in stone. But like the kittens who had been raised to see only horizontal lines, I had been raised to see only that I could be second with someone, never first. I didn't believe I was lovable and valuable, or that I deserved to be loved. I didn't believe I could have the love that I wanted.

I want someone to love me the most, I said. *I want to be first with someone. All my life I've been second, or third, or eighth. I could get into the* Guinness Book of World Records *for being runner up. Finalist. Semi Finalist.*

Birth order. And you were a difficult child. Oversensitive, terrified, inquisitive.

So I've heard. And I suppose you think Dad was right, and it was my fault you died.

No. Your father was wrong to say that. He was angry that I had died. He shouldn't have taken it out on you. But you have to face all that. You have to forgive him. It wasn't about you.

It's not about me.

You have to let go.

I have to let you go. This is where I let you go.

My mother got out of the car. She reached into the back seat and lifted out my camera bag. Then there was a very brilliant flash of blue light; afterward she was gone.

Define Paradox

A FTER THE BLAST, Elaine got out of the car, but I sat there for a long time, listening to the painful hum in the air. It reminded me of the time when I was nine and I refused to go into a local drugstore with my mother, because of a high pitched screeching sound she couldn't hear. She didn't believe me until a store clerk told her it was a burglar alarm that most dogs and a few children were particularly sensitive to.

I watched the workers from the black pearl farms running back and forth from their various buildings with their carts and dogs. One of their dogs was lying on the ground dead, another was barking at something it thought it saw in a singed coconut tree. But there was nothing in the tree. I wondered if it was barking at the painful humming noise, or something else, some other damage, that we were too old and too human to see or hear.

Elaine opened the driver door. She asked me to get out of the car and wait with her by the lagoon. We could hear megaphone noise again, but could not understand what anyone was saying. The car-radio no longer worked. Once, after my car blew up on the freeway, my father said I was too calm in emergencies, and did not react swiftly enough. As I got out of the car and followed Elaine to the lagoon, I wondered if this were one of those times.

At the water's edge we watched the waves lap, and the dead fish, mollusks and eels beach up. Elaine was afraid of a tidal wave, but the explosion had not been detonated in the water. Elaine held out her hands. *Somehow I didn't really believe they would do this,* she said.

People do all sorts of things.

So this is it? Elaine said.

What?

Your nightmare. Your landscape of rain and fire. It wasn't in the past after all. It was in the future. But where's your mother?

She was in the car. Where were you?

I was in the car.

No. She was in the car.

Elaine shook her head. *I told you,* she said, *it's like hockey—you can knock the other person out of position.*

The sky was clearing on Mururoa. We waited for Larkelon's boat to pick us up. Elaine said: *I know there is a poison here now, but I can't see it.* While we waited, the fog cleared. The sunset was purple and yellow. I remembered that Matatea had once said that what we call fog, is really the *kohu,* the mist.

There she is, Elaine said, pointing out into the water. *There's your mother.*

My mother arrived, driving a small motorboat. She looked at me and Elaine, but said nothing. We smiled at her but pretended to the others that we didn't know her. We climbed into the boat, as did many of the pearl farm workers. They carried the dogs in their arms, both dead and living, and some chickens in baskets. The ride into the lagoon was quiet. Everyone looked stunned. We had all spent weeks preparing for this to happen and yet no one believed it had happened. My mother dropped the pearl farm workers off at various larger boats that would take them out to sea and away from the radioactive fallout. She left Elaine and me at Larkelon's boat. She never spoke, and no one spoke to her. I wondered how I could say goodbye to her and let her go if she kept reappearing. But then I realized that was the truth of it, the paradox of it. I had to let her go, even though she kept reappearing.

On the way back to Kosrae, everyone sighed and looked blankly out to sea, except Matatea and Larkelon, who smiled and said we had stopped the nuclear testing for good. *Why does it require another tragedy to stop this?* I said. *There have already been so many.* Larkelon shrugged.

Not any tragedy will do, Elaine said. *A tragedy has to be properly timed to effect change. This one may have been.*

A well-timed tragedy, I said. *What a concept.*

Elaine said that, in *The Wizard of Oz*, Dorothy and her cohorts fall asleep in the poppy field on their way to the Emerald City, because the wicked witch had drugged them. It takes white snow falling on them from the good witch of the north to wake them up. I asked Elaine why she was telling me this. She said because I had a dream about my father taking me to the airport in his army uniform in a white car, a flight that was delayed by a snowstorm.

What are you telling me?

Wake up. And run to safety in the Emerald City. That's what I'm telling you.

Art is the lie that tells the truth.

A mystery wrapped in an enigma.

Obscurity is not profundity.

Happiness is not the absence of pain. Pain does not equal damage.

Touché, I said. I was wide awake. I was sure of it.

When we returned to Kosrae I insisted we stop at the house in Walung before going up to the sanctuary. I told Larkelon I needed to rest, but I didn't need to rest as much as I needed to go home. Have you ever come home after a trip, and you've been so changed by your experiences that although you've only been gone for weeks or months, you feel that you've been gone for years? That was how I felt when I walked up the steps into the house and back to the studio, like I'd been gone for years and years, and was finally returning home.

Since I could not travel as fast as the others, Matatea decided to take Elaine up to the temple sanctuary first, and Larkelon and I would follow more slowly. I said I did not know why we had to go at all, why we had to hide. Who would come after us? So many people were responsible. There were so many to question or interview. Larkelon said that no one else had a mother who had been in the FBI during the

Marshall Islands testing, or who had admitted the Americans' part in over exposing the islanders there.

I had witnessed, and I would tell my story. He said there would be a time to talk publicly about that, but that time had not come yet. Matatea said that I needed to trust her, that there was a reason to go to the sanctuary that was beyond safety, beyond respite, beyond timing, and that I would not understand what it was until long after I had been there.

I told her I had not trusted anyone since my mother died, but I would try.

She told me on the contrary, I had trusted Elaine and the others to travel with me around the islands, I had trusted Larkelon to show me the islands, and now I needed to trust again.

The way up through the basalt canyon to the sanctuary was steep, but filled with beauty. There were enormous red flowers with soft draping petals that grew in vines along the canyon walls. The river that ran through the canyon was always changing—sometimes it looked more like a creek or a stream, sometimes it was wide and full and raged. There were waterfalls and pools in other places where we stopped to drink or bathe or rest. One pool was filled with giant eels, and in another there was a swirling center that shiny bronze fish jumped out of. At night, phosphorescence flew from tree to tree. Larkelon said it had been identified as a kind of fungus. I asked Larkelon if this canyon was a magical place.

Very.

I asked him if it was a dangerous place.

All magic is dangerous.

I asked him how we protected ourselves against danger.

You watch. You wait. You trust your instincts. Then, when it is time to act, you act. But you always protect yourself.

How do you protect yourself?

You did it the way you protected anyone else; you shielded yourself from danger.

How do you know the danger is coming? What if you're blindsided?

He shrugged. He repeated himself. He said: *You watch, you wait; you trust your instincts.* He thought people were rarely blindsided. But they often weren't cautious, weren't watching. Or they didn't trust their instincts.

I wasn't cautious. So I told him I loved him.

He told me that we were *riliko*, or cross cousins. He explained that my father was his grandmother's brother, or *jibo, rikora.*

My father? Which father?

On the last day, I felt I was coming to a place I had been before. *You have been here before*, Larkelon said. I thought perhaps it was my vision then that I had come here in my mind. That I had seen this place in my mind, but he said it was not like that at all. *Not everything happens only in your mind. Some things are happening right here.* He tapped his finger on the air, as if it were solid.

There were stone steps leading up to the sanctuary, three gateways, and lining the path, a profusion of the red flowers I had so admired deeper in the canyon. The sky was a bright azure streaked with navy, and when I looked down the mountainside I saw that the ocean below was the same. I knew this must be the place.

We used the southern entrance to the sanctuary. There were more stone steps and two lions on either side. They each had one paw slightly raised, and they had their mouths open in a curious curled way, like an elephant. It was as if they were laughing.

Larkelon motioned for me to ascend the stairs in front of him. He came in and stood behind me and turned me around. It was then that I had my *frisson* of recognition, that I saw, finally and definitively, and without a doubt, the doorway in my vision. I was standing on the sandstone floor. The terracotta pot with the yucca plant in it was to my left. Looking out over the densely foliated hillside, I could see the ocean beyond, azure with navy streaks. It was hard to tell where the sky ended and the water began. This was the place I had been searching for all along.

I spent my days in the sanctuary looking out at the ocean below, looking out at the view from the doorways. I could have stayed there forever and just looked. I had never felt contentment. Now I knew it was this: this view, this feeling of joy at doing exactly what I was doing, at doing nothing. The feeling of rightness with the world. This feeling of certainty, as if there were no doubt. Sometimes my old restlessness came back, and I wanted to take a long walk out there, in the trees and underbrush, out of sight of the temple and the ocean and the sky. Take a long walk in the past and the future, in my old fears and worries.

But Matatea said I could not go out there alone, because it was not safe. She said I did not know anymore who I was. I did not know my way and I might get lost. *Come with me, then,* I said, but she said it was not really safe for her either. *But you brought us here. You know exactly who you are.* She acknowledged that she brought us there, but said it was not the same as going for a walk. Then she said that none of us know exactly who we are.

I know who I am, I said. *I'm a sculptor and photographer and I live in California and I'm lonely and homesick and I'm afraid of everything and full of doubts. I came here so I would lose my fear and start living again, but now that I'm going home again I'm afraid I've accomplished nothing by coming.*

That's not who you are, Matatea said. *That's what you do.*

Well then, who am I?

Matatea laughed. *You don't have the faintest idea who you are, apart from what you do, do you?*

No. I haven't the faintest idea. Certainly I was not without qualities. I had many. On the less fortunate side, I was impatient, immoderate, nervous, fearful, conflict avoidant. On the more fortunate side I was imaginative, inquisitive, supportive, nurturing, gentle, whimsical, childlike, impish, kind, loving, strong, competent, efficient, logical. But was that who I was? The sum of my qualities? Who was I?

Matatea asked me to imagine the self that I was no matter what happened, no matter if I was fat or thin, happy or sad, successful or unsuccessful, loved or unloved, fearful or fearless, in pain or out of pain, restless or content, empty or full, in the desert or at the beach, in the city or the country, alone or with people, tense or relaxed. *Do you know that person?* she said.

Yes, I know that person. I know her very well.

That is who you are.

I asked her about my birth father. Matatea said that my birth father was a storyboard artist. He had lived in the house in Walung after my mother and Karlat had returned to the States. He had died only a few years before I came. He knew how to read the rongorongo boards. Matatea said he taught me how to read them when I was a child, and if someone put a rongorongo board in front of me I could read it. She showed me a picture of one. On it there were pictures of fish, birds, hunters, a fetus developing.

How could they see a fetus developing? Elaine said. *Did they have ultrasound technology through the moon people? Did they practice abortion?*

Matatea smiled mysteriously at her. Larkelon said that in some island cultures you can read a person's life through their tattoos, some through rongorongo boards, some through story boards.

Matatea called me Tohunga. I thought it was a nickname, until Larkelon explained to me that it meant the *adept class*. The *adept class* studied astronomy. I wondered what else my birth father had taught me, and what I had inherited. I was studying geography. And language. Rakaru was the name of a volcano on the southeast corner of Easter Island. It was also the name of an islet in the Arno Atoll in the Marshall Islands. What was the connection? Polynesian legend said they launched seven canoes from the high island of Raiatea, and that is how the Pacific Islands from Easter Island to Hawaii to New Zealand were populated.

Since these islands were all volcanic, it made sense that each atoll was the rim of its submerged volcano, and each high island has a volcano in the interior. The high and low islands were actually the inverse of each other. Tahiti has Mt. Aorai. Bora Bora had Mt. Otemanu. Raiatea had Mt. Temehani. Tinian had Mt. Lasso. It made sense that if the volcanoes were sacred, then the lagoon was sacred, since it was the mouth of the volcano, and that the shrines were on the mountain tops, for they were the tops of the volcano. It made sense that the royal dwelling should be made of prismatic basalt, because prismatic basalt was crystallized lava. When something crystallizes in your mind, what happens? It becomes clear.

The Easter Islanders said they came from Marae Ranga in the northwest. *Mararanga* means northwest. Did they come from the Tuamotus? *Marae* also means temple. What else does *Ranga* mean? A female rongo? What is rongo? A rongorongo board is a story board. Is ranga a female story? What is the female story? The waning of the male moon?

The floor of the temple was sandstone bricks. Large ones. I liked to run my hands over the cool, smooth stone, fitted together like the walls at Machu Picchu. Elaine said I was a sensualist and otherwise clueless, and I did not know what I was doing. I asked if there were sandstone on the islands. Matatea said a lot of materials on the islands were imported, and that the laughing lions and the temple seemed to be made out of the same stone. She told me that there was a bay in Moorea called the Sea of the Moon. Elaine asked me if maybe that was where the moon people were from. I asked her what did Stonehenge, the Machu Picchu, the palace at Knossos, the palace at Nan Matol and the giant stone faces at Easter Island have in common?

Roo sprang from his mother's flank. Rona is the woman in the moon.

The circular stone structures, what did they represent? The islets in an atoll? The volcanic rim? The shape of a spacecraft? A distant planet? The circle of life? A nebulae? When I lay down inside the temple with my head and shoulders outside, and the rest of me inside, and I swung my arms and legs, I knew that there was no limit to the world. I knew that I could fly. Elaine said I looked like a turtle swimming. The sacred turtles at Nan Matol, the prismatic basalt city—were they swimming, or flying?

I told Elaine that in these islands, the West is to the east, and the East is to the west. Here everything was inverted. High volcanic islands and submerged volcanic atolls were inversions of each other. These islands were the hinge of the world, the pivot point, the moment of interpenetration, the paradox, the sacred place.

Was Crete the opposite seam? The other pivot point? The flip side of the coin? Where all of the west is to the west and all of the east is to the east? The Minoans the inverse of the ancient Pacific Islanders? I had been comparing the symbols on the rongorongo boards to those on the Minoan story coins. They were not the same, but they were similar. On the rongorongo boards the story unraveled in a switchback fashion, like a trail down a hill, or a meandering stream. On the Minoan story coins, the story unraveled in a spiral, like a snail shell, or a whirl wind, or a black hole, or a tornado. But the Bikinians settled their island in 1500 B.C. so they could have known the Minoans. If they could sail that far. I believed both of them could.

Elaine asked me to define paradox.

A paradox is something that seems contradictory, but is really complementary.

She asked me to define interpenetration. I told her to imagine two mirrors facing each other. If you looked inside them, you would see rings of multiple inter reflections, spiraling deeper and deeper into the mirror, into infinity, into a point where the rings are so small we can't see them anymore.

Matatea said that when you are out in the ocean and the water and sky are moving around the boat, instead of the boat moving, that was interpenetration.

So it is, I said.

You thought you were looking into your past, Elaine said, *but you were really looking into your future.*

Your past and your future, simultaneously, Matatea said.

So I was, I said.

That's inverted, Elaine said.

So it is, I said.

Aunt Charlotte brought our food to the temple. She smiled at me, and laughed. She laughed and pointed with Matatea. When I was flying from the temple doorways, she put her hand on my back, so I would not fall from the sky, she said, and hurt myself. Sometimes she would sit beside me, and stroke my arm or my hair, quite lovingly. Sometimes she would put her palm against my cheek and cock her head to one side, and smile. Sometimes she gently removed the hair from my eyes with her fingertips.

She said I must love myself fiercely, protectively, and unconditionally the way a mother loves her child. She said I must believe that I'm valuable, lovable and deserve to be loved, otherwise I would keep chasing after love and esteem from people who couldn't love or esteem me, instead of accepting love and esteem from people who could give it freely.

I told her that I was left-handed and most left-handed people had lost an identical twin in the womb. I wondered if I had lost a twin. I thought this explained why I felt like a very small child. Aunt Charlotte said that was not why. She said that when you learn to love yourself you return to your original nature, and that was why you felt like a small child. But I did not believe her.

I did not believe anyone anymore. I had entered into a profound state of total disbelief. I felt free. I could see everything. I could see the sky beyond this sky. And the sky beyond that. And the sky beyond that.

What does your soul imagine? My soul imagines a white sand beach, a clear blue sky, and me floating on my back, my head above the water. I am happy. I do not feel pain. I do not feel fear. I feel loved.

Happiness is not the absence of pain. Pain does not equal damage.

Aunt Charlotte said I needed to learn to contain my desires, let them fill me up, before I released them. She said I was too impatient. I agreed with her; impatience was my worst quality. I couldn't stand suspense. I couldn't stand the feeling of containing anything, letting anything in. She said that was why I wouldn't let anyone love me.

Elaine went out with Larkelon and brought back art supplies from my studio in the house in Walung: paint, clay, canvas. She said that we were going back to California soon. She said that she had all my unfinished pieces from my studios in New York and on Cape Cod shipped to California, and all my work at the house in Walung had also been shipped. She said Sandy had rented me my old apartment in Santa Cruz and was getting my old studio back, and that by the time we got there, everything would be in place, and all the artwork would have arrived.

I said: *But what if I don't want to go back, what if I want to stay here?* Elaine said I didn't understand, she wasn't taking me back to the east coast, to New York or Cape Cod. I didn't have to go back there. She was taking me back to the west coast. To California. To Santa Cruz. She was taking me home.

And give up my teaching job in upstate New York?

You hate your job in upstate New York.

She was right. I liked the students but I avoided the politics, so I wasn't going to meetings, which was part of the job. And now I was AWOL. I was going to get fired anyway.

How will I make money? How will I support myself? I wanted to work in a photo lab, but the standing and lifting aggravated my back. People thought I should do commissions or decorative work, but again, I couldn't control the conditions and so it was more likely I would aggravate my back.

You'll find a way, Elaine said.

But I just paid off my debt from my back surgery.

All the more reason to go home.

But I couldn't support myself there before. I couldn't find enough work. I didn't have health insurance. I was going deeper and deeper in debt. That's why I took the teaching job in upstate New York in the first place.

Things are different now. You're out of debt. You've saved enough money to move back. The economy is better. You're changing.

I'm changing?

How much easier can we make it? We can't find you a job. You have to learn to take normal risks again, instead of going to the extremes of taking no risk at all, or taking the monumental risk of exposing yourself to a nuclear test. I scowled at her. *You have to learn to take normal risks again,* Elaine repeated. *That's what living is.*

But all I could think about was how I hurt my back, I couldn't work for two years, I went into debt, it took me ten years to climb out of debt, I had lost everyone I loved, and I couldn't hold down a job. Risk was supposed to be calculated. Risk was supposed to be something you did when there was a high likelihood of success. I, on the other hand, was always flirting with catastrophe and losing. I smirked at her.

Elaine said: *You have to learn that taking a risk doesn't automatically mean disaster. The safest place to do that is home, where you feel happy and confident.*

I said: *I had a dream, and you and you and you were there, and if you ever go looking for your heart's desire, you needn't look any farther than your own back yard, because it was there all along.*

That's right. Home.

But I am in my own backyard.

Matatea said that Kosrae was my birth father's home, but California was my home. She said I should go home to California for a while. That I needed to go home. She said if after I went home for a while, if I wanted to come back again to visit, that was alright with everyone in Walung.

On my smaller canvases I painted the view from each of the three doorways. On my larger canvases I painted the murals from Knossos: scenes of irises and dolphins and men and women with broad shoulders, narrow hips and long thin legs carrying terracotta pots and playing with each other's hair. Elaine thought it looked Minoan. With the clay I made tiny replicas of the terracotta pots with the yucca plants inside. Elaine said they were not yucca but palm. Matatea would not settle the argument.

Making progress? Elaine said.

I told her I didn't know. Working on a sculpture or painting or series of photographs for me had always been like solving a problem. Progress came in stages. I was never sure what I was searching for. I only had an intuition. Insight came suddenly, when I least expected it, after I'd pushed and pushed, and then given up in despair. Then I'd be having coffee, or doing laundry, and an idea would come to me. *Evrika!* I've found it! It was always the most obvious insight; one I felt I should have known all along.

On the last canvas I wanted to paint the landscape of rain and fire. Elaine asked me what that was. I told her that Bikini was a landscape of rain and fire. Enewetok was a landscape of rain and fire. Mururoa was a landscape of rain and fire. Love was a landscape of rain and fire. Loss was a landscape of rain and fire. Happiness was a landscape of rain and fire. Pain was a landscape of rain and fire. Fear was a landscape of rain and fire. Grief was a landscape of rain and fire. The universe was a landscape of rain and fire.

But how do you paint that? Elaine said.

I don't know, I said, and I began to weep.

Why Are You Here?

I DID NOT WANT to say goodbye to Larkelon, Matatea, the temple, my life in the temple, my life on Kosrae. If I could be homesick for the place I was leaving and the place I was going simultaneously, then what was homesickness? And was it a sickness? Or simply a longing?

Before we left Kosrae I insisted we stop in Walung again so I could say goodbye to my birth father's house. I had lived there not knowing it was his house. I had never known my birth father, and now he was dead. Matatea said I knew my birth father very well, because I was very much like my birth father. She said I had his childlikeness, his curiosity, his languor, his love of the ocean, his love of telling stories through pictures, his love of fruit and shellfish, his love of art. She said I had his laugh and his smile. She said I had not lost him, because he was inside me. She said I would not lose Kosrae, because it was inside me.

Everything you've ever been and ever known, ever felt and ever seen, ever wished and ever dreamed is all inside you, Matatea said. *You don't lose it.*

The house in Walung was the same as it had been when we had stopped at it on our way to the sanctuary, except that my artwork and other belongings had been removed. But in a way it was not the same, because now I understood it was my birth father's home, and had always been so. I said goodbye to the house in Walung, by placing the enormous red flowers, with their huge voluptuous petals, in the corners of every room. Then I lifted my arms and repeated my benediction again and again, looking up to the ceiling and down to the floor, up to the ceiling and down to the floor, over and over in each room: *Love and you will be happy. Be mysterious and you will be happy.*

Eventually my birth father appeared, holding one of the flowers. He embraced me. I looked just like him, except that I was lighter skinned, and not so wise.

Why are you here? I asked.

You were calling me.

I was? I started to cry.

Sit down. I did. He sat down with me. *I want you to keep crying, until all the pain is out.*

That could take several days.

We'll wait.

We did. I cried and cried. Sometimes I'd go out on the porch and cry, and look at the waves breaking. Sometimes he would feed me, or put me to bed, or into the shower.

I think I cried for three or four days. Elaine says it was two weeks, but I don't think dead people have a very accurate sense of time.

When I finally stopped crying I said: *Why didn't I do this before?*

Because you never had a safe place, my birth father said. *First you had to confront your mother, your Aunt Charlotte, Andrew and Elaine. A wound has to close before it can heal.*

I asked him why I had always been afraid, from before I could even remember.

You were conceived and born in the apocalyptic landscape of nuclear blasts. Nothing could be more threatening to a child's sense of personal security. Of course, you are afraid. Who wouldn't be? You carry that with you always.

That's the whole reason why?

You're oversensitive. You see things people don't see, sense things people don't sense, feel things people don't feel, dream things people don't dream, know things people don't know. It makes you afraid. Who wouldn't be?

I'd rather not be, I said quietly. *Do I have to be?*

There's nothing we can do about that now. He put his hand on the top of my head like a blessing.

I asked him if he could teach me what he knew. He said he could. So my return was postponed while my birth father taught me to read the rongorongo boards. Then he told me I had to go back home.

This is my home, I said.

This is your ancestral home. Your home is in Santa Cruz.

Can you come with me?

No. But I will always been with you.

Home

E LAINE RENTED A car when we arrived in Los Angeles. I insisted we rent a white one. I also insisted we drive up the coast. I did not think I could be away from the coast for very long. Elaine drove. We didn't really talk. When we arrived in Santa Cruz I could not really believe it. I said so.

Why not? Elaine said. *You always planned to move back here. Throughout your years teaching in upstate New York you always said you would move back here.*

I never believed I really could move back here. I never believed I could have what I wanted.

Well believe it, Elaine said, as we pulled into my apartment complex next to Lighthouse Field and the cliffs above the ocean.

For the first few weeks after I got back, I didn't do much. Mainly I walked down the block from my apartment to the cliffs, and stared out at the ocean and the horizon. A few times a week I drove up the coast to Davenport Landing, a natural harbor that had originally been used for whaling ten miles north of Santa Cruz, or to San Gregorio, or to one of the beaches in between. At the beach I would sit in the sand and make these circular structures out of rocks, like Stonehenge, or little rock huts that I called maraes. Sometimes I would fill them with flowers I had brought with me, usually the orange nasturtiums, yellow mustard flowers, and white lilies that grew wild along the cliffs above the beach in Santa Cruz.

During that first month back, Sandy checked on me weekly. She kept reminding me that as the nuclear protester whose FBI agent mother had admitted U.S. guilt and responsibility for exposing the islanders to nuclear radiation during the 50s testing, I had a month of interviews and talk shows to do; but she promised she wouldn't schedule them until I told her I was ready.

After the Mururoa blast there had been an international outcry over the incident, the UN had gotten involved, and as a result the Polynesians had called an emergency election. The independence party had won, voting in Oscar Temaru. The French were preparing to withdraw completely from Polynesia the way the British were going to withdraw from Hong Kong in the summer of 1997. The process would take two years.

The United States Congress had scheduled another oversight hearing into the Marshall Islands cleanup and reparations. Larkelon had submitted many of his suggestions, combined with my own, through one of the Marshallese government representatives, asking for complete restoration of the islands, including a radiation-free environment, an end to nuclear waste dumping, economic independence, complete medical care, full disclosure, and return of Bikinians to their atoll within one year. They were even asking for their organs back from the Mayo Clinic in Rochester.

Larkelon thought a lot of progress had been made in exposing the dangers of testing, but he still needed me to tell the story of what I had witnessed. He said it would make the Americans and Europeans aware of what was going on, and force them to take responsibility for the past and stop any testing in the future.

I told Sandy that I might be ready in a week or two to do the interviews. I kept thinking about what Larkelon had said: that I must witness, and then I must tell my story. That it would make a difference. I hoped he was right.

Sandy had been taking care of my phone calls so I could have some quiet the first few weeks back in Santa Cruz. She told me that, in addition to the journalists, gallery owners were calling and asking to show my work. We talked about how the incident might end up making me a famous artist after all, how ironic that was, whether or not I was ready to face the public both politically and artistically, whether or not I was ready for career success.

They'll attack you, Sandy said. *They'll tell lies about you. You have to be ready.*

I told her I wasn't ready to be treated like I was important, especially in such a negative way. I didn't feel important. I felt like I always had, small and unnoticeable, someone who blended into the landscape without making a mark.

A few weeks after we returned home, Larkelon sent me a package from Kosrae, and another anonymous package arrived from Mr. Tom Wong's black pearl farm on Mururoa. I sat down with both packages on the futon couch near the sliding door. I could see the ocean a block away, and hear the seals barking and waves breaking. I opened Larkelon's package first.

It was an audiotape. I played it. There was a lot of static, but over that I could hear: *I'll get you out of here, I'll get you out of here. I asked you to face your fears not run headlong into suicidal danger. But you were waving from the different shores.—I was waving you away, motioning to you to go back.—I thought spirits couldn't cross the water.—You've gone from extreme avoidance to monumental recklessness.—I love you—I have to let you go. This is where I let you go.* After that the static stopped and there was only a soft humming as the tape spun around in circles.

I opened the package from Mr. Tom Wong's Black Pearl Farms. I found my cameras inside, along with two packets of developed film. I looked at the photographs. They showed the orange sky, the fog over the lagoon, the rainbow, the flayed fish, the birds with their wings on fire, the flaming coconuts and bananas falling to the ground, the black pearl farm workers running with their carts and shouting, my face as I gripped the wheel in the unmoving car. But I found no photographs of Elaine or my mother.

And You and You
and You Were There

THE STUDIO WAS just a few miles north of my beach apartment, in the hills on Western Avenue, overlooking an undeveloped canyon where a family of wild cougars lived. To drive to my studio, I took a long, circuitous route along the cliffs above the ocean, to the end of town, where the Natural Bridges beach park begins. Then I drove inland, around the park, the university's dolphin research facility, the Wrigley Gum and Lipton Tea factories, Silicon Systems, and several health food plants. From there I crossed the coast highway and head north on Western Avenue toward the university campus. After some track houses, condos and an apartment complex the view opened out to the west on an undeveloped canyon. My studio was in the cottage off a house overlooking this canyon.

Sandy and I had put my clay tools and photography supplies back where we remembered them. The darkroom was the same. What was new was the work I had been doing. We had set the new terracotta sculptures of a half-reclining woman based on Aunt Charlotte, and the half-reclining man based on Andrew, near the sliding glass door overlooking the canyon. They looked different than I remembered them on Cape Cod, more whimsical, more ironic, more playful, more unreal. The paintings of the doorway vision we had propped up on a work counter underneath the high north window. The colors looked deeper and more arresting than I remembered. And the painting of the dolphins and irises looked like the embodiment of the joy I felt when I was home.

I had been home a month before I went to my studio really determined to work again. On that day I found Andrew out on the porch, smoking a Gauloise and drinking Glenlivet on ice. I went out to him. *You shouldn't smoke out here,* I told him, *There's a high fire danger in this canyon.*

Hello beautiful.

I thought you weren't coming back.

I came to model. I want you to be able to finish. He came inside and laid down on the couch. I wheeled his unfinished figure into position and wet the clay with towels.

So did you find what you were looking for? he said.

I found the nightmare, the vision. I smirked at him.

So what's the problem?

I'm still afraid.

Maybe there's a reason. Maybe you'll always be afraid. Maybe you'll learn to tolerate it or even like it.

Maybe.

My back doctors had two gauges of pain tolerance: how much you felt the pain and how much you minded it. Maybe my fear was similar, and the degree to which I felt the fear and minded it would diminish to a level I could tolerate. But the fear wouldn't go away. Not completely. Not like in the temple sanctuary when I felt like I could fly.

Are you going to come back regularly? I asked.

Just today.

That's what you said last time.

We can't imagine the future. We only know right now.

I envy you.

He sat quite still for several hours, and I worked without interruption, without thinking. Afterward he smoked another cigarette, fixed himself another Glenlivet on ice (he took the bottle from my refrigerator) and looked at the doorway vision paintings, and the dolphin and iris painting.

This dolphin and iris painting would make a nice mural, he said.

It is a mural. In the palace at Knossos.

He nodded. I rubbed my hands on his chest and kissed his neck. I wondered when my desire to bring back the dead would leave me, and I would be content. After we made love he left his drink on the counter and kissed me on the forehead. *I have to say goodbye,* he said. He looked out the window to where the sun was setting.

That's what you always say, I told him. Then I said: *Why couldn't I be the one for you?*

There was no one for me. I was too afraid to let anyone close to me after my wife was murdered and Duane committed suicide. But if there had been someone for me, it could have been you.

I Learn to Build a Container for the Heart Song. I Teach Myself to Fly.

WHEN I WENT back to the studio early the next morning, Aunt Charlotte was waiting for me, stretched out on the modeling couch.

You can finish now, darling, she said.

So I see.

Are you feeling better?

Much better.

Then I realized the yellow jackets had fallen out of their nest and stung me again, and I cried and cried, and I asked myself if I was in pain. No, I wasn't in pain—I was just afraid. I had learned to separate fear and pain.

Happiness is not the absence of pain.

Pain does not equal damage.

I wheeled the unfinished block of clay over, wet it with towels and began. Aunt Charlotte remained motionless for several hours and I worked without interruptions. When I couldn't work anymore I went and sat down on the couch beside her.

I'll always love you, I told her.

She told me that was all right. It was all right to love. *Love and you will be happy,* she said.

Karlat. Bekka, Bekka. Aunt Charlotte fell asleep. I must have fallen asleep too, on the other modeling couch.

Sandy called during dinner. I told her I was almost ready for the interviews and the galleries. I told her that people had always told me that success would come to me only when it no longer mattered, and now I finally believed it might be true.

You almost seem content now, she said.

I am. Why shouldn't I be? I wished I could accept it when I wasn't content. I knew that time would come again. Unfolding and enfolding.

What an odd situation, Sandy said. *To be content. Is it frightening?*

Yes. Terrifying.

And people will hate you. From envy.

Probably, I said. There was a silence on the other end of the line. *Maybe it won't last long. Maybe I won't get a gallery, my pieces won't sell, and I'll have to work at some terrible job like before, leave Santa Cruz, have no time to do my artwork. I'll never get back to Kosrae.*

Any of that could happen, Sandy said. *Would it be worse than before?*

Both better and worse, simultaneously.

I was beginning to be able to tolerate the paradox, contain the tension between the opposing poles. It was like tuning a guitar: if you wound the string too tightly, it would break. If you tuned it too loose, it would not play. I had always wound my strings too tight or too loose. I was trying to balance the tension perfectly now, so my heart could sing.

We got off the phone. I went back to the dinner table. Aunt Charlotte asked me if I remembered the blast. I nodded. Of course I remembered the blast. I remembered every second of it. The low ominous sound right before. The rumbling. Then the shaking. The brightly illuminated sky. The rain falling. The ground opening up. Flaming debris falling from the sky. People and carts running in every direction. My hands as I gripped the wheel. The landscape of rain and fire.

I wish I could have saved her, I said. Oh how I wished I could have saved her.

You mother? You couldn't have saved her.

Not even from cancer?

How can a twelve year-old save her mother from cancer?

It was your memory, wasn't it? I said.

What?

The landscape of rain and fire. It was you driving the car. I was you in the dream. You rescued her.

Yes, she said. *I was still in the Navy. We saved each other.*

So the memory was both past and future.

Yes.

Were there people, animals and carts running in all directions?

Yes.

Did you drive her out of there in a white car?

Yes.

And did you say: I'll get you out of here, I'll get you out of here?

Yes.

I knew it.

You're so smart.

I rolled my eyes at her. *I'm not smart,* I said. *If I were smart I would know how to support myself financially, my artwork would be shown and sold, I'd be in a satisfying relationship.*

You know how to fly, she said.

I laughed. *That's true. I do know how to fly. That's the one thing I know how to do. Perhaps the only thing I know how to do.*

I want you to teach me how to fly.

Now?

First, I'll model for you, and you'll finish your sculpture.

And eventually you'll leave. And I'll paint the landscape of rain and fire.

Yes. The landscape of rain and fire.

I did what Aunt Charlotte suggested. I finished the sculpture. I taught her how to fly. Afterwards I said: *You are my biological mother, aren't you. My mother is really my adoptive mother. She raised me as her own daughter because I had an island father, and you didn't want my uncle, your husband to know. That's why Dad was always so impatient with me. That's why I was your favorite growing up, and not my mom's or my dad's. That's why you wanted to take me back after Mom died. You left your apartment to Ben because he'd nursed you through your last illness and because you didn't want anyone to ever suspect. That's what I lost. That's what I'm not supposed to know.*

You're so smart, Aunt Charlotte repeated. She kissed me. *Will you hate me now?*

How could I hate you? You've always been my greatest source of love and comfort. You've always been my only source of unconditional love.

When Aunt Charlotte had gone, I shut my eyes and imagined the landscape of rain and fire. I was in the driver's seat of the car, my adoptive mother and my birth mother were in the passenger seat. I had my hands on the wheel and I was saying: *It's time for me to let you go. This is where I let you go.* My adoptive mother put her hand on my face. She turned and got her overnight bag out of the back seat. My birth mother opened the car door, kissed me, and they both got out. My adoptive mother put her bag down, looked up at the sky, and brushed a wisp of hair out of her face. They took each other's hands. Then the bright light came down to them and they were gone. When the brightness faded I was at the cliffs over the ocean.

I got out of the car and walked uphill along the cliff edge, until I found the adobe doorway with the terracotta pot in the entrance. I went inside. The room was completely empty, except that there were drawings on the walls of dolphins, and irises, and people carrying pots and playing with each other's hair.

From the inside I turned around and looked out. I was very high up. If I peered out far enough I could see where the cliff dropped down to the beach below. The sky and water both had navy and azure streaks; it was difficult to discern where the sky ended and the water began. I lay down on my stomach in the doorway and swung my arms and legs out into the air. I wasn't afraid. I knew that I was flying.

Acknowledgements

I could not have written this book, or any of my other books, without the early support of a Wallace Stegner Fellowship at Stanford University, a National Endowment for the Arts Grant, a Fine Arts Work Center Provincetown Fellowship, and writer's residencies at the MacDowell Colony, Yaddo, Millay Colony, the Djerassi Foundation, Montalvo Center for the Arts and the Margo Gelb Dune Shack through the Outer Cape Residency Consortium. These gifts have lasted a lifetime. Special thanks go to Paul Nelson for his ongoing encouragement. Thank you to the University of Lynchburg for their support, and the University at Albany, for their gift of a Writing Semester, Fall 1997, and library resources, both of which enabled me to research and write this book. The "you and you and you were there" dialogue sections (pg. 166) are paraphrased from memory of the 1939 film version of the *Wizard of Oz*, from MGM, from the book by L. Frank Baum.

About the Author

Laura Marello is the author of six published works: novels *Claiming Kin, The Tenants of the Hotel Biron, Maniac Drifter,* and *Gauguin's Moon;* story collection *The Gender of Inanimate Objects;* and poetry chapbook *Balzac's Robe.* She has been a Stegner Fellow, Fine Arts Work Center Fellow and recipient of a National Endowment for the Arts grant, a Vogelstein grant and a Deming Grant. Marello grew up in New York and Los Angeles. She studied poetry with Ray Carver at the University of California Santa Cruz and Ed Dorn at the University of Colorado Boulder. She studied fiction with Gil Sorrentino at Stanford University and Padja Hejmadi at CU Boulder. Marello just completed a novel about three women lighthouse keepers on the central California coast, and is beginning a memoir about the confluence of nature, spirituality and friendship in the desert of the Coachella Valley.

Printed by Imprimerie Gauvin
Gatineau, Québec